From a Vine

a novel by

Michelle Cushing

MULBERRY🌳BARK

A MULBERRY BARK BOOK
Published by
Mulberry Bark Publishing

Copyright © 2007 Michelle Cushing
Cover photography copyright © 2007 XT Photography

All rights reserved. No part of this book may be reproduced or transmitted in any form or by any means, electronic or mechanical, including photocopying, recording, or by any information storage and retrieval system, without the written permission of the Publisher, except where permitted by law.

For information contact Mulberry Bark Publishing.
http://www.mulberrybark.com

ISBN: 978-0-9796935-2-6

Printed in the United States of America

First Edition

MULBERRY🌳BARK

For Grace & Pepper

Treasure is peculiar. Sometimes we don't have to dig.

The fingers of the ceramic praying hands pointed upward like a pyramid, holding prophecy like an Egyptian temple. Lightly, she touched her fingertips to those of the small statue before stepping out onto the porch. Sashaying and seducing her into the yard, the trees and flowers swayed in the breeze. With so many gardens, the yard looked like a grass mural splattered with yellows, purples, and reds. Around the house she went, stopping to smell each bloom. The home had a breathtaking scent to accompany the view.

Such joy here, she thought and smiled.

She retrieved her watering can and gave the plants one last sprinkle. The water drops sat atop each blossom and bud, almost standing at attention, giving her a salute. Loving the smell of water mixing with dirt, she took a deep breath.

Her heart lurched.

Stumbling inside, she found her way to her room, opened a drawer beside her bed, and removed the program from her husband's funeral. Yellowed around the edges, now looking almost like papyrus, the writing on the paper told only a portion of the story. While the paper had grown old, her memory of the day was as ripe in her mind as a seedling emerging from the dirt to glimpse sunlight for the first time. As she turned the paper over, she couldn't believe their season together had been over for so long. Spring would come again, she knew that, and warmth filled her breast. She flushed like an autumn leaf turning from green to red. Like an orchid plucked to make vanilla, life did not end but began anew with something just as sweet.

She put the program away and pulled out a small tattered bag. After undoing the ribbon, even though she knew the contents very well, she took one last look inside. From her pocket she removed two small items and dropped them into the bag.

"True love is easy to grow," she said quietly and glanced at her husband's photo still at her bedside. "But first you have to plant it."

Feeling a pain in her chest, but not being afraid, she hurried back to the praying hands.

Chapter 1

Sweet Olive

There had to be something worth keeping. Joy kept digging. Something. Anything. Dirt covered the past, held her future. In the present, it revealed nothing. She fell back on the ground, not caring that her sweaty hair mixed with the freshly upturned dirt and made little clumps of mud at the back of her neck. She squashed a clod of earth in her right hand. "Just junk," she whispered.

The diamond mine had recently opened after the mayor saw it as an opportunity to create a tourist trap. So far, one tourist passing through had found a diamond – not a big one, but a diamond nonetheless. Today was Joy's first visit and she had utterly enjoyed it. Unlike others, she didn't necessarily have to find a diamond to be happy. Almost anything she found was buried treasure to her. She loved the feel of the earth. She loved to dig into it and feel the life and history it held. It was almost spiritual. Even as a child, she had loved to get dirty. She would roll in the freshly plowed ground while her father tilled away on his tractor. Sitting there with a clump of dirt in her hand, she'd wonder what had been there before. She wanted to keep digging and digging and digging. The dirt would never end and that thrilled her. Joy could discover forever.

Opening her compact mirror, she wiped a smear of mud from under her eye. After tucking a strand of hair behind her ear and stretching her arms, she gathered her things. Dirt covered her book bag and she shook it off vigorously. Although she rather liked the dusty look – it reminded her of something rugged from *Indiana Jones* – her mother would not approve of a dirty book bag tracking mud into the house. She slung the bag over her shoulder and a pen flung out. Sticking into the soft dirt, the pen pointed upward. Her gaze followed its direction to a gathering of pine trees swaying in the light breeze. She picked up the pen, cleaned it off, and stuck it back into her bag.

"Stupid zipper," she muttered, referring to the broken one on the front of her bag.

As she hurried home, her sandals clacked on the cement sidewalk, popping back up to smack her in the heel. Her next shoe purchase would definitely be sandals with a strap behind the heel. Sweat started to pour down her face and her book bag felt like a boulder strapped to her shoulder. A truck honked as it drove by and a large, bearded man leaned out of the window to whistle at her. Joy kept her head down and frowned. Idiot, she thought, glancing up to read the truck's bumper sticker before it sped away. As much as she loved Wenton, Georgia, the life there made no sense to her. Everyone in town followed the unwritten rules: go to school, perhaps community college or trade school, then get married and raise a family. Joy knew there was more to life than merely existing, more to be seen, more to be learned. She believed life was meant to be explored, and she didn't understand the town motto that came straight off a bumper sticker on a beat-up, pickup truck: "Life sucks then you die."

When she finally arrived home out of breath, she stomped up the porch steps, threw open the door and exclaimed, "Somebody shoot me!"

"Where have you been?" asked Joy's mother, Beverly, a real estate agent with short blond hair and a model's face at forty-eight. "Why are you so dirty?"

"Diamond mine. Didn't I tell you I was stopping by after class?" Joy dropped her book bag on the chair where her father used to sit. His vacant spot near the television was rarely noticed anymore. The bag landed near the tear on the chair's arm, tugging at the gray duct tape. Joy was the culprit who had ripped the chair when she was ten years old by pretending to be a pirate. Over the years her father, pounding the arm and yelling during Cowboy football games, had stretched the tear into a large, gaping hole.

"Right. I forgot. I'm a ditz." She playfully bopped Joy on the behind with her newspaper. "We ordered pizza. There's some in the fridge."

"Great. I'll get some later."

"How was day one?"

Joy sat down next to her book bag. "Fine. Weird to be in school in June, though. Geology was interesting. I had to buy some topographical maps, which were a little expensive. Geography shouldn't be too hard."

"That's good, hon. Only till December and you'll have your associate's degree. Excited?"

"Then I have to go to a university for my bachelor's." Joy rolled her eyes and got up to head for the shower.

"Joy ... "

Joy shook her head. "Mom, we've been through this."

"I know, sweetie, but it's so expensive."

"I have plenty of money that Dad left. That's why he left it. Do we have to go through it again?"

Beverly straightened her newspaper and folded it neatly. "No," she said.

Joy left the living room and walked down the hallway, passing by her little sister Katie's bedroom. Katie, fifteen, was slumped in a beanbag chair with headphones over her puffed, frizzy blond hair, which was transparent against the silent, illuminated television. Katie's Sony Walkman made a screeching sound like all portable radios that are turned up too loud. "Child's gonna end up deaf," Joy muttered to herself.

Emily, Joy's 28-year-old sister, nodded as she walked by with a cordless phone. "Of course, Jonathan. Yes, dear, it's a great choice for Saturday night. Is that movie still playing? You know I love Stallone," Emily said into the receiver, twirling the ends of her short brown hair.

"Since when?" Joy wanted to know. Emily pushed her sister away.

Joy opened her bedroom door and flopped down on the bed. The cool cotton comforter felt good against her outstretched arms and she sighed. She could hear Emily giggling at her fiancé on the other end of the phone. "Really. Somebody shoot me!" Joy said once more. She rolled her eyes, took a deep breath, and slid off the bed like a drunken person too tired to stagger out of a bar. Walking over to her dresser, she arched her back until it popped. The dresser top was littered with pencils, notebooks, old soda cans, and tipped-over picture frames. The drawers were stuffed beyond maximum capacity and her Garfield nightshirt, so old it had a small hole in the shoulder seam, stuck out at the top and kept the drawer from closing. Without even bothering to open the drawer, Joy yanked out the nightshirt. She stuffed down the rest of the clothes and tried to push the drawer closed. It wouldn't budge. Joy smirked and threw the nightshirt over her shoulder. She took off her silver heart necklace that her father had given to her mother; it was inscribed "Simon and Bev forever." Joy dropped it with the rest of the clutter on the dresser.

Staring into the mirror, she noticed that her long brown hair had turned kinky from the heat. The ends were soaked, so she pulled a wet strand into her mouth and sucked off the salty sweat. She grimaced because her face, with its dark brown eyes and perky nose, showed her exhaustion. Her skin was greasy from the sweat and her cheeks sunk in from the heat. She sucked the last drops of sweat from the strand of hair and pushed it away with her tongue.

Joy opened the middle drawer and began a search for clean underwear. The tag on a new bra rubbed against her hand as she rummaged through the heap. She pulled the bra out and held it up; it dangled from her hand like a large slingshot. "Well, this definitely isn't mine." She tossed it over her shoulder. Through the mirror, she saw it land near the trash can. "Good shot." She arched her thin frame again and turned to get a sideways look at herself. She held up her breasts, squeezed and repositioned them. "Too small?" she pondered. "No, average." She smiled.

"What the hell are you doing?" Katie asked, standing in the doorway.

"Don't you ever knock? Get out!" Joy threw the nightshirt at her sister.

"Hey, that's what locks're for. You should've shut the damn thing," Katie said in her heavy Southern drawl. She bent over, picked up the nightshirt, and threw it back. "By the way, squeezing them won't make them grow." The nightshirt hit Joy in the face.

"Whatever. You think I want cantaloupes like yours?"

"Jealous?" Katie cocked her head and held up her breasts.

Joy rolled her eyes. "Oh, yeah, way jealous. I guess that's why you're so spacey. Having those things knock you in the face when you run can't be good for you." Joy threw back her head and laughed like Cruella DeVil in *101 Dalmatians*. "And," she added, pointing her finger at Katie, "I've noticed you've been wearing a lot of baggy shirts lately. Better lay off the junk food, honey."

Katie curled her lip. "Do you want the bathroom, or not? You really smell."

"Yeah, don't go in there." Again, Joy pointed her finger at Katie. "You'd be in there all night." She continued her search for underwear, while Katie stood in the doorway watching. "By the way, Katie, that's your bra over by the trash. Mom must've put it in here by mistake."

Katie walked over and picked up the bra, inspecting the tag. "Yeah, this ain't yours."

"Incidentally, why so courteous to offer the bathroom to me first?" Joy asked.

"I just said you really smell."

"Really?" Joy sniffed her shirt.

Katie chuckled. "Actually, I feel sorry for old people. Seeing you there staring in the mirror. Sad, really. That's it for you. This is your body. Twenty years old – you've passed puberty and started on the decline. What else do you have to look forward to?"

"Your numerous venereal diseases."

Katie's face went blank, silent as Mount Rushmore, wanting to speak but covered in cold stone. "Well, at least there's a possibility that I could get one," she said, finally stumbling on a comeback as she left the room and slammed the door behind her.

"Slut," Joy muttered.

She jerked out a pair of panties, wadded them up in her hand, and headed for the bathroom.

Emily squatted in the hallway, still on the phone with Jonathan. "Jon, we couldn't do something so crazy ... " Emily said, then cupped the receiver as Joy walked by. "This is private."

"Hallways are public domain. Why don't you just go to your room?"

"Sorry, Jon. No privacy around here."

"Tell me about it." Joy sighed.

When Joy got to the bathroom, she sat down on the floor and started picking the burrs from her socks. Earlier in the day before going to the diamond mine, she had done a little exploring in the woods behind her house. As a child, she had followed the trails on various adventures. The trails still remained, but some of the passageways were grown over with stickers, vines, and bushes. Plucking out the burrs made her think of her childhood. Many times her father had held her on his lap to pick out the little stickers that she had gathered from a hard day of prospecting. Once she tumbled down a particularly prickly hillside, and her father had to pull burrs out of her stringy, matted hair.

"Joy Bear, someday you gonna pull me a dinosaur bone outta all this exploring?" he had asked her.

"No, Daddy! A whole dinosaur!" Her dirty feet had dangled from his lap and swung back and forth. "And, I'll ride him up to the house!"

"You will?"

"Yeah, he'll do all your work for you 'round the farm. Then you can watch General Hospital with Mommy."

"Why would an old man like me want to watch soap operas?" He had rubbed her head, while she pondered the question for a minute.

"There're pretty girls on it."

He had laughed loudly. "When I have your mother right here!"

Joy had put her hand over her mouth. "Oops."

Thinking back on the memory, she chuckled. Her parents seemed to have had a perfect marriage. Still, her father once told her that most people didn't believe it would last. Beverly was twenty years younger than Simon Baxter. Joy reckoned all the other guys her father's age must have been jealous, as Beverly Williams was a truly gorgeous, right-off-the-pages-of-Cosmo beauty. Without a stitch of plastic surgery, she had maintained her slender frame and creaseless face over the years. Only now did she show a hint of crow's feet, easily concealed with makeup.

After her shower, Joy returned to her room to scan her new textbooks. Her rolled-up geological maps sat in a corner of her room. Directly after school, she had taken them home before going to the diamond mine. She didn't want them to get dirty. She cleared off the top of her desk and spread out the maps. Glancing over the terrain of Georgia, her eyes stopped briefly at Atlanta, then quickly ran to the edges of the map. Soon they wandered to the window that was framed outside by a sweet olive plant. The fragrance from the little white blooms was so strong that it scented Joy's room from outdoors. Luckily, her mother hadn't noticed that it had grown so big, so it remained for Joy to admire. Night had fallen and the stars were out like an army to watch over the planets. She gazed at them for a while, then opened her desk drawer and pulled out course books from several universities. Many of them had come with letters of acceptance. Her grades were excellent and she was free to choose almost any school she wanted. A professor from the University of Texas at San Antonio had even offered to let her go on a student archeological dig in the coming spring. Still, she wasn't sure what she would choose. Part of her regretted having gone to community college, but her mother had convinced her that she wasn't ready to leave home yet.

"Think about being out there all by yourself," Beverly had said to her. "It's dangerous. What if something happened? You got sick? I couldn't come and get you." At eighteen, that had made sense.

As Joy flipped through the pages of the University of Memphis course book, her mother knocked on the door.

"Come in," Joy said without turning away from the listing of anthropology classes.

"Would you like some iced tea, dear? I'm making a pitcher."

Joy turned around and smiled. "Sure." For Joy, the sweeter the tea, the better.

"Did you get any pizza?"

"I'll get some in a minute."

"What are you looking at?"

"Course books."

"Oh." Her mother closed the door.

Joy frowned and closed the book. She left the maps unrolled on the desk, but put the course books back in the drawer. Leaving her bedroom, she thought of the future and sighed at the doldrums of life.

Her sisters were sitting at the table, while her mother reclined against the counter, waiting for the tea to boil. Joy opened the refrigerator and lifted the lid of the pizza box. Mushrooms and sausage. She gagged at the thought of eating a fungus. "Why'd you get mushrooms?"

"Katie ordered it," Beverly replied. "I guess she forgot about your aversion to mushrooms."

"She did it to spite me," Joy muttered under her breath.

"Pick 'em off," Katie replied with a grin.

Instead of pizza, she opened the freezer and pulled out a cherry popsicle. She still felt flushed from being in the sun all day. The cold treat would cool her down.

"How was school, kid?" Emily asked. "You haven't said much about it."

"Fine. Nothing too strenuous."

"Bobby called for you while I was on the phone with Jon. I got his new number," Emily told her and smiled. "He's moved into his own place now."

Joy ignored her and unwrapped the popsicle.

"Aren't you going to call him back?" Emily asked.

"Whatever."

"I suppose he wanted a date, dear," her mother said and spooned sugar into the empty pitcher. "You know he's been dying to go out with you. Call him back. Don't be rude. Besides, it'd be nice to see you go out for a change instead of staying home wrapped up in your studies."

"Or in the woods digging up shit," Katie said.

"I hear you've been spending some time in the woods of late. Of course, you weren't alone out there," Joy shot back. Katie huffed and shut up.

"Girls, don't start," Beverly said, pouring the boiling water into the pitcher. "You don't want to go out with Bobby?"

"Not interested."

Beverly added more water to the pitcher and stirred. "Why not, dear? I hear he drives a rig for Coke now. Makes good money. I saw his mom recently."

Joy put up her hand like a traffic cop. "Really, I'm not interested."

Emily sighed. "I know. The only thing that can stop you from achieving your dreams is a man. Stupid theory."

"Good theory." Joy balled up the popsicle wrapper and left the kitchen to go outside. It wasn't that she didn't want a boyfriend; she wasn't interested in the merchandise that surrounded her. The shelves were lined with row after row of the same box with the same contents. Just once Joy would like to see a gold box among the gray touting a list of rare ingredients.

"You should go for him, Joy," Katie yelled after her. "Not many men would want a scarred woman like you." The tiny scar above her lip was Joy's sensitive spot. She had received it in a tire-swing accident when she was twelve. To most people it was invisible, but to Joy it stuck out like a red shirt in a pile of white laundry.

"Katherine," her mother whispered.

Joy stopped in the living room, picked up her boom box, and went outside. Even in the late evening, the heat in the small, sweltering town of Wenton was almost unbearable. Joy sat on the porch swing and listened to dogs barking in the distance before she flipped on her CD player. As she scanned to the right song, the sweat started to roll down her clean face, and the red popsicle juice slid down the side of her hand. She licked off the juice just as the song began. Jackie Wilson pleaded "why" as Joy reclined, her right leg curled underneath her, while her left foot rocked the rickety swing. If she listened closely – although she didn't care to – she could hear the beer-drinking, hardworking, country-music themes that governed the town. The tall pines blocked most of the sounds, but she could still hear an occasional child playing somewhere near her half suburban and half middle-of-nowhere home.

She finished her popsicle and snapped the stick in half. Even though she was barefoot, and even though she had on only a nightshirt, she had a strong urge to run behind her house, through the woods, and all the way up to the old Madson house. As Jackie Wilson crooned about tears in his eyes, Joy swung slowly and chewed on the inside of her mouth. December, she thought, it'll all be over, then I can leave.

She swatted at the mosquitoes that swooped down to snack on

her arm. After biting her, the insects returned to the porch light, which was also covered with fluttering moths. The insects looked like a mound of darkness as they clamored hopelessly toward a light that was not the true sun. Surveying the sky, Joy popped out the compact disc and stretched her slender frame, trying to relieve the nightmarish things the swing did to her back. As she picked up her boom box to go indoors, the porch creaked and more paint chipped off the wooden planks. "Really needs a paint job." She pulled off a long strip of white paint and tossed it into the yard, which was covered in wild flowers, mostly dandelions that her mother was always trying to kill. A breeze caught the hem of her nightshirt and beckoned her to step into the yard. She obeyed. Her bare feet crushing the soft grass, she strolled toward the oak tree that still had the tire swing hanging from its limb. Joy kicked the root that jutted from the ground and had caused her scar. I'm too big for you now and you can't hurt me, she thought, rubbing her big toe. Picking one of the flowers and examining it, barely able to make out all its parts in the dark, she held it up in the moonlight, then carried it inside.

Chapter 2

Cross Vine

New York Times; April 2, 1992

Efram T. Corbet, 32, one of America's hottest artists, will unveil his latest works at the Crystal Ballroom Gallery in Manhattan on Saturday.

"This will be his last show for a while. Mr. Corbet feels it is time to leave New York and search for motivation," Patrick Bullock, Corbet's publicist, said in a recent statement.

"I love New York. It has been my home for fourteen years, but I think I have lost the sheer joy of painting. Why am I painting? I have to find that again. I need a quieter place without a hectic lifestyle, so I can create," Corbet said.

Corbet will be present at the invitation-only event. The exhibit will be open to the public on April 5.

Efram refolded the newspaper clipping and stuck it back in the pocket of his black Armani slacks. He pulled out a note to his publicist that contained a list of numbers, a small message, and a magazine photo stuck to the note with tape. While he contemplated putting something else on the note, a myriad of celebrities, artists, critics, and reporters roamed the rooms of the gallery, munching on costly hors d'oeuvres and drinking expensive champagne. They ogled the paintings like livestock to be haggled over. For the most part, as Efram sat alone in a corner sipping Evian, they didn't bother him. Occasionally a "dahling," as he liked to call them, would walk by to congratulate him, and Efram would smile curtly, raising only one side of his mouth. Some of the regulars he liked socializing with, those who seemed to grasp what he was trying to do with his work. An *Art News* critic had once told Efram his paintings were the closest thing to God on canvas. That was the only time Efram had ever felt modest about his work.

Stuffing a loose strand back into his long black ponytail, he listened as two art buyers explained and debated his work. Efram leaned back as far as the chair would let him and tapped his head repeatedly against the wall. He loved showing his work but hated art shows. His only reward was spying on the unsuspecting, then confronting them like poison ivy – unassuming but with a nasty itch.

"Still nothing but a nineties version of Victorian decorative art," said one buyer, who looked like a blast from Andy Warhol's era, goatee and all. Efram could picture him beating on a drum in a coffee house and repeating the phrase "Cool, man."

"Yes, and I thought Maxfield Parrish died in the late sixties," said the other buyer in a heavy British accent. To Efram, he looked like Patrick Stewart with a potbelly.

Efram laughed under his breath as the two continued to discuss the painting in terms that meant nothing. After running his hand over his hair to make sure it was in place, he got up and approached the two men.

"Excuse me, but I think you have it all wrong," Efram said and stole a cheese puff from the English buyer's plate. "What exactly does all that gibberish mean, and does it have anything to do with art?" He popped the cheese puff into his mouth.

"Pardon? You're an expert, I suppose? I'd love to – ahem – hear your interpretation. Quite interesting, I'm sure," the English buyer said. He raised his eyebrows and waited for Efram's response.

Efram took a few sips of Evian before handing the glass to a waitress walking by. "May I?" He pointed to the other buyer's napkin. Before he could respond, Efram removed it from his plate. "Well, it's merely a painting of a woman, a beautiful woman, reading a book under a tree. Do you see her face? So content. You can almost hear the silence of her reading that book. You can almost guess what the book is about."

"Nonsense," the English buyer interrupted. "What does *that* mean? Who cares? Take a snapshot."

"Are there any Efram Corbet paintings you do like?" Efram asked.

The other buyer chimed in. "Well, I'll tell you that Efram Corbet used to be a great artist. This Victorian stuff was great when he started, but he refuses to change."

"Sell out?" Efram asked, raising his eyebrows.

"Sell out! Good heavens! He *is* a sell out," exclaimed the English buyer. He leaned over and whispered to Efram, "Two hundred and fifty thousand dollars for this one, mind you! And this is one of the cheaper ones! Who's selling out? Bloody insane!"

Efram chewed on his bottom lip. "Uh-huh." The napkin was still in his hand, twisted. "If you hate his work, why are you here? This is an art show. People come here to buy art."

The man hesitated. "I'm here to inquire ... for a friend, you see ... "

"Uh-huh." Efram raised his eyebrows again.

The other buyer jumped in. "Well, I'll tell you he did something a few years back that was quite brilliant. It was called – oh, I think it was *I'm Bored* – and it represented the ... "

"Oh, yes, yes," the English buyer cut in, "the one with the beautiful use of red and blue just splashed across the page and the yellow circle in the center?"

"Yes, it was marvelous. It represented the meaning of life and all the monotony. Fabulous. *I'm Bored*. What a great title," the buyer responded and giggled.

"Maybe it meant he was bored?" Efram said. "Maybe it was an artist's doodle and nothing more?"

Both buyers looked perplexed.

"Jamie said a few losers with too much money and not enough intellect would love it. I think that painting sold for half a million," Efram said and checked the time on his Rolex.

"Jamie? The curator? You know her?" The English buyer snapped his fingers, pointed at Efram, then nodded his head. "You hang the paintings, don't you?" All three men roared with laughter.

Efram lightly patted him on the cheek. "I'm the artist." The chuckling ceased. Efram dabbed the corners of his mouth and put the napkin back on the man's plate.

The two men huffed and walked away.

"Well, there's one missed sale," Efram said to himself. "Bummer for me." He snapped his fingers. "Gotta find Patrick. Where is he tonight? Damn! He better be here. I don't care if ... "

"Efram! Efram! Efram Corbet! I've been looking all over for you, you little wallflower, you!" shouted a flamboyant reporter for one of New York's trendiest art 'zines. "Is this really your last fling?"

"Fling?"

"New York night life won't be the same without you." He laughed. "So, what's the scoop?"

"No scoop, Rich. Just want to get out of here. It's like everything I do is in vain. Look at all the people here tonight. Do they care about my paintings? They don't see what I see. I'll tell you what they do see – dollar signs."

"Touché." The reporter took out his notepad to jot down Efram's words.

"Bye, Rich." Efram waved and started to walk away. "I don't want an interview."

"Oh, come on. A few more questions. I saw Cindy Adams over by the buffet table. You know she'll sniff you out eventually. I don't want that old broad scooping me, much as I love her."

"One more quote," Efram said. Rich smiled and flipped open his notepad. "What kind of world is it when people think they have the right to analyze my work, but they can't recognize me in person?"

Rich shrugged. "You're not exactly Michael Jackson."

Efram smirked.

"Oh, come now, we all get our little egos bruised now and then."

Efram shook his head. "How do these people get on the guest list?"

"I don't know. Maybe they won some big art lottery or something."

Efram laughed. "The world of art is commercialized then." He shook Rich's hand. "Hey, I gotta run. Thanks, Rich."

Efram began his search for Patrick, only to be stopped by a woman in her sixties with heavy makeup, a gold jacket, and enough jewelry to brighten a lighthouse.

"Excuse me, are you Mr. Corbet? Dear, it's marvelous what you can do. Tell me, could you do a portrait of me for my husband? Your paintings are so sensual, so full of passion. I'd love for you to capture that for me." She rapidly blinked her heavy eyelashes and grinned.

"Madam, I am not for hire. Who the hell do you think I am? If you want one of my paintings, choose one from the walls." He walked away, leaving the woman standing there, gaping. "This is driving me nuts," he muttered. The hospital-white corridors of the gallery made him feel as if he were in an insane asylum. Everywhere, his own paintings looked back at him. When he reached his favorite in the new collection, a portrait of a woman standing on a balcony staring up at the sunrise, he stopped. A painted cross vine weaved around the edges of the portrait, the orange flowers clinging to the side of the apartment building, framing the sky, then slinking like a snake back down to the bottom where it almost pushed the woman's foot off the ledge. Efram knew the woman in the painting. Early one morning he had glanced out of his apartment window and caught her leaning on her balcony rail next door. He had opened his window and yelled, "Whatcha thinking about, Maxine?"

She had replied, "Endless possibilities," and continued to lean against the railing and stare into the sky.

"Don't move," he had urged her. "I want to sketch you, if you don't mind?"

She had giggled and put her hand over her mouth. "Why not. Maybe I'll be famous some day."

Efram then set up his easel on his balcony and sketched her for several hours. A month later he painted the portrait on canvas, each morning paying Maxine to stand on her balcony.

He was lost in remembrance when a blond woman wearing a full-length blue beaded evening gown approached him. "Lovely painting."

"Thanks."

"Thanks? So you're the notorious Efram Corbet?"

"In the flesh." He shook her hand.

"You have lovely paintings."

"Thanks again."

"So, does this painting have some deep meaning, or is it just a nice picture? I don't understand art too much. My husband over there has to explain things to me." She pointed to the English buyer that Efram had already dealt with.

"Well, I can tell you those silly pseudo-intellectual phrases mean nothing. I don't put them in my work. You want to know what this painting symbolizes? See, it's like she has her back to the world and her mind on all types of possibilities. See how her foot rests on the bottom of the railing? Looks like she's about to lift up and leap off there. She's not trapped or restrained in any way. Nothing is impossible and everything is amazing. That's what I wanted to capture. Period." He reached across the maroon security rope and an alarm went off. Several burly security men bolted toward them. The woman jumped back as Efram nonchalantly pulled the painting from the wall. One of the officers yelled for him to stop and tried to grab the painting.

Socialites gasped and reporters fumbled for notebooks as Efram held the painting above his head. Hearing the commotion, Jamie, a tiny woman with bobbed brown hair and wire-rimmed glasses, sprinted down the hallway. Her high-heeled shoes clicked on the marble floor. "Good heavens!" she shrieked and glared at Efram. "What in the name of all that is sane are you doing?"

"This one isn't for sale." Efram proceeded to make his way out of the gallery.

"What do you mean, it isn't for sale?"

"I called it *Mine*, so you see it's ... you get the picture. I mean, I get the picture. Ha!"

"Efram, we had an agreement." The edges of her mouth curled under like hot plastic.

"Reach in my pocket."

"I beg your pardon?"

"There's a note for Patrick. Damn him. I don't think he even showed up tonight." Efram walked on through the gallery, ignoring all the stares.

Jamie kept her head down. "There was a movie premiere in Los

Angeles. Stallone, I think."

"Shit. Some friend he is. Give him the note, then tell him he's fired. I can find a better publicist. Damn Hollywood publicists. Snobby as fucking hell anyway. Tell him to give the note to Marlon. Marlon can do it."

Standing in front of Efram to keep the photographers from taking a picture, Jamie reached into his pocket, pulled out the note, and opened it. "What's it mean?"

"I saw a house in a real estate magazine. That's it." Efram nodded. "Tell Marlon to check on it for me. I think that's the one I want. It's in Georgia."

A reporter stopped Efram and shoved a tape recorder into his face. "Why did you decide to keep this one? What does it mean to you?"

"It means I forgot something." He walked away, leaving the reporter and the rest of the guests dumfounded. He stepped into the foggy night air with one thought on his mind: I've got to get out of here.

Chapter 3

Dandelions

"I sold the estate!" Beverly yelled, as she threw open the door. A chorus of "Yea!" and "Whoohoo!" followed as her three daughters hugged her. "Under my supreme sales skill, the Madson estate has been purchased for two hundred thousand dollars! Thank you. Thank you!" Beverly bowed.

The sale was a major coup for Joy's family. Beverly, who had never worked, took a job as receptionist for Gold Star Real Estate after her husband died of a heart attack. After making small talk with a well-to-do client that led to a million-dollar business deal, Beverly was promoted to sales assistant, and within five years became the top agent in the company. This position did not, however, afford the family every little comfort of life. Emily contributed her wages as a clerical worker in a doctor's office to the family income. Katie worked at a local dairy bar, but was allowed to keep her earnings for the important expenses of teenage abandon. Joy survived on student-loan money and a small inheritance left by her father in a college trust fund.

As Joy returned to shucking corn in the kitchen, she asked, "So, who bought it?"

"Some artist guy from New York. I never met him. Dealt with his agent. He videotaped the property back in April and over-nighted the tapes to the guy. I honestly thought he wasn't interested, since it's been so long. Well, I guess he liked what he saw. Bought it without even seeing it in person. Corbet's his name. Efram Corbet."

Emily poured boiling tea into a glass pitcher and stirred. "I remember seeing some guy filming around town. Shooting the strangest stuff, like Brooke's Grocery, the bank, the drive-in."

"Saw him, too," Joy said. "I was wondering who he was."

"Short bald guy?" Beverly asked, placing her briefcase and a brown paper shopping bag on the floor. A box from the bakery, she placed on the table.

"Yeah," Joy and Emily replied at the same time.

"Inch, pinch, owe me a Coke," Emily joked with Joy for saying the same word.

"What kind of artist?" Katie asked, trying to pry into the bakery box. Her mother lightly slapped her hand.

"One with money. Who else would be that nonchalant about money to buy something sight unseen?"

"What's in the box, Ma?" Katie sat down at the table and slowly pulled the bakery box closer.

"Celebration dessert!" Beverly opened the box and pulled out a cherry cheesecake. "Looks good, doesn't it?" Everyone nodded. Beverly placed the cheesecake in the center of the table, then went to the stove to sniff the spaghetti sauce. She lifted the lid on the steaming pot. "How is it?"

"I added some more oregano. Made it a lot better," Emily answered, spooning some out for her mother to taste.

"Delicious," Beverly said. "So, the biscuits done yet?"

"Uh-oh!" Katie yelled and jumped up to check on her job. Carelessly ignoring her duties had left the biscuits flat and charred on the bottom. Katie frowned.

"Don't lag behind, kid. This is suppose to be a well-oiled machine," Beverly said, patting Katie on the back.

Joy broke the corn in half and dropped it into the boiling water. Well-oiled, monotonous, and boring, she thought to herself, yawning, and put the lid on the pot.

"How was school? Day two any harder?" Beverly asked.

Joy shrugged and sat down at the table to check out the dessert for herself. She stuck her finger in the side, scooped up some frosting, and licked it off her finger. "So, what's in the grocery bag on the floor?"

"Oh, I got something to kill those damn dandelions sprouting all over the place," Beverly answered, kicking off her Payless pumps.

Joy didn't understand her mother's preoccupation with killing the alleged weeds. "Can't kill them. They go where they want. Free spirits," she said.

"They don't belong here," Beverly responded, rubbing her toes.

Emily, continually stirring the sauce, asked, "So, when's this guy moving in?"

"In about two weeks."

There was a part of Joy that was sad to see a new person moving into the house. It seemed it would forever be the Madson house to her. Mrs. Madson had only been dead a year, and Joy didn't like the idea of someone being so nonchalant about buying the house. It wasn't property to her. She had spent half her childhood at that house, especially in the summertime when the swaying willow trees kept her nice and cool. All the children in town loved to come by and frolic in the lake. Joy was no exception, but most of the time she was the leader of an expedition. Typically dressed in pink cut-off shorts and T-shirt, usually dirty, she would stand on the large tree stump in front of the house and announce that Indians had lived in the area many years ago, leaving behind buried treasure and priceless artifacts. She would lead the kids all over the yard and into the surrounding woods and trails, the archeological dig taking on a frenzied pace as each one tried to find a historic treasure. Her sweaty, scraggly, uncombed hair pulled back in a loose ponytail, Joy would inspect each child's find and usually throw it over her shoulder and say, "Just junk. You've got to dig deeper." If the find looked noteworthy, Joy would announce, "I've got to take this back to the lab for more research." Some days she would bring the object back to the kid who found it and give a drawn-out explanation about a "Paleolithic, Jurassic, Parthenon artifact." Mostly, though, she kept the treasures for herself and amassed a huge pile of junk, from rocks that resembled arrowheads to "ancient" bottle caps that she often flung at her older sister's Barbie collection.

Gracie Madson, a round little woman with gray hair pulled up in a bun, had kept the grounds covered in plants and flowers. The magnolias loomed large and the flowers still bloomed after all the hard work she had put into the gardens for over fifty years. The estate looked like something from a Monet painting, slightly hazy and impressionistic. The white house was settled back far enough not to disturb the serenity, but stood out enough to resemble a magnificent castle to any child still young enough to let her imagination get the best of her.

Joy loved the openness of the house with its many windows and its big wrap-around porch. The hardwood floors glistened as the sunlight poured in at every opportunity. The furnishings were modest and many. Paintings hung on the walls and books lined the many shelves. It was a house that was quiet, but with plenty of space left for music. Mrs. Madson often filled the house with tunes, whatever was popular at the time, for the many children who dropped by to taste her delicious peanut butter cookies and apple turnovers. As a child, Joy popped by almost daily after school. She knew Mrs. Madson would fill her a Dixie cup with Coke and hand her a s'more on a paper napkin. Joy, delighted with her treat, would then skip past Mr. Madson, a spirited little guy with a bald patch covered in age spots and a pipe constantly hanging from his lips. Joy knew Mr. and Mrs. Madson had a relationship like a rocking chair, solid, comfortable, and relaxing. Mr. Madson would wink at Joy and she'd giggle. Then Mrs. Madson would hurry Joy and the other children into the den and turn on the record player, so they could all dance.

The only thing about the house that bothered Joy was the ceramic praying hands that reached out to God. Standing on a dark wooden desk next to the front door, the hands acted as a guard. Joy had no choice but to face them after a long day of play if she wanted to retrieve her shoes, which Mrs. Madson always placed near the desk. Joy figured the praying hands were holy and feared committing a mortal sin if she stood beside them without praying herself. She usually tried to fake-out God by running past as if she didn't know they were there. The house, Joy thought, even smelled of a Bible that had been through many generations of families, not musty but earthy, with a sense of belonging attached to it.

Now, it belonged to Efram Corbet. A man she'd never met.

"Two weeks, you say?" Joy asked, still digging into the sides of the cheesecake.

"Yep. Why'd you drop the corn in so late? Everything else's done," her mother responded, frowning.

Joy ignored her.

Chapter 4

Honeysuckle

F or the most part, Efram enjoyed the one-hour drive from Atlanta to Wenton. His black Porsche convertible had been waiting for him in a hangar when he stepped off the plane from JFK. "The perks of fame, eh?" he remarked to the attendant. He had contemplated driving all the way from New York, but decided against it when he realized his gray Chinese pug, Mr. Boogie, probably wouldn't enjoy such a long car trip. The drive from Atlanta sufficed for Efram. It brought back memories of his mother driving him to Memphis from Little Rock when he was a child. He liked passing the endless fields, the rundown farmland, the cattle, the old barns, and the tourist-trap novelty stores that hocked everything from oversized wagon wheels to homemade preserves. Efram bought a few jars of preserves, something he hadn't eaten since he was a child. During the summer, his mother used to make grape and strawberry jellies, along with Efram's favorite, muscadine jam. He had gathered the berries in the woods behind his Arkansas house.

Billboards also entertained Efram on his way to his new home. Not only did the signs let him know that food and fuel were only minutes away, they gave him a game to play. With each one he passed, he tried to imagine the billboard coming to life. One ad featured a woman holding a bottle of maple syrup; Efram pictured her stirring an earthenware bowl of pancake mix, pouring it on a hot skillet, then kissing her son on the cheek. Another ad showed a family dining at Casey's Fine Southern Grill. The little boy's smile in the ad was covered with barbecue sauce. Efram imagined the boy sitting behind a tree, after making off with a bowl full of cookie dough to eat for dessert. After passing too many beer ads, however, he stopped the game.

Most of the time during the trip, he played loud music, mostly soul from the 1960s, his favorite. He also listened to some jazz, a little classical, and when he was alone on a long stretch of highway, disco. His voice going as high as nature allowed, Efram sang the words to disco classics.

Occasionally, he stopped and took some pictures. "Hey, what *are* those things anyway, Mr. Boogie? Cotton gins or something?" He pulled over and reached into the back seat for his camera. Watching for traffic, he got out of the car. Adjusting his lens, he muttered, "Cool, whatever you are." Then he climbed back in the car and continued on his drive, waiting for the next cool thing to appear.

A stop for gas just a few miles out of Wenton gave Efram a chance to see what the town might be like. "Time for gas, Boog. Getting hungry? How 'bout a nice doggie treat?" Mr. Boogie kept his head over the edge of the convertible's door, his tongue flapping in the breeze.

Efram pulled into a station with a bright red Coke sign above a screen door that barely held on to its hinges. The rusty pumps looked like something from a 1950s commercial, minus the spick-and-span tidiness, with round tops and a counter that flipped the numbers over.

Efram looked around and saw two faces staring at him through the screen door. "Probably wondering whether or not I'm queer," he muttered to himself. He nodded. Politely, the faces nodded back. Efram cracked a smile. "I guess they're open. You stay. I'll get you something." The dog sat down, wagging his tail. Efram reached into the back seat and pulled out two Kleenex. He got out of the car and put the tissues in his palm to remove the dirty handle on the pump. The smell of gas caused him to wrinkle his nose. The numbers clicked over, slowly, while Efram struggled to keep the pump from jerking. "Damn this." After pumping the gas, he wadded up the tissues and chucked them in the waste basket.

The door of the station creaked open and Efram stepped into the musty room. The air conditioning was serving up cool, petroleum-scented air. Old license plates hung on the walls, along with new and used parts. An old man behind the counter, who wore a gray work shirt with "Burt" embroidered above the pocket, asked, "How much?" He had the heaviest Southern accent Efram had ever heard. Keeping his hands in his pockets and leaning against the counter, a blond teenage boy eyed Efram.

"Fifteen, but I'm going to get a drink." Efram walked over to the cooler and put his hand into the ice. He felt like dipping his head in it. His Levi's were sticking to his thighs and his T-shirt was becoming sheer.

"Nice car," the teenager said, molesting Efram's Porsche with his eyes.

Efram removed a Sunkist from the cooler. "Thanks. You got Evian? For my dog." He pointed to the car.

"Naw," the man said and scratched his sunburned nose, peeling off dead skin. "None that fancy bottled water stuff."

"Well, I think I have enough to get to Wenton. Maybe I better get him a Pepsi just in case. He's kinda partial to Pepsi." Efram laughed, grabbed another drink, and walked down the aisles, which were almost barren, and surveyed the available treats. "You got anything granola?"

"Naw," the man replied again and folded his arms.

"How about beef jerky? Dog again." Efram pointed with his thumb over his shoulder.

The man nodded. "Down et tha end."

Efram walked to the end and picked up a Snickers bar, the only thing that looked fresh. He inspected the expiration date, then examined the beef jerky dates.

"You not from 'round here are ya?" the man asked, rubbing his scruffy beard.

Efram wrinkled his forehead, one eyebrow rising higher than the other. Is this a movie or something? he thought. "Uh, no, I'm going to Wenton to be hung for a crime I didn't commit." The old man sucked on his teeth while the boy grinned.

Efram walked back to the counter and put down his items. "You know the Community Way exit?" Efram asked and opened the Sunkist.

"By the college," the boy said. "Are you going to school there?"

Efram smirked and took a big swig of his soda. "Do I look that young?"

Taking his hands out of his pockets, the teen asked, "Um, can I look at your car? She's sweet."

"So I'm on the right path?" Efram asked the man.

"Yeah. Which way ya headed?"

"Cedar Hill," Efram said and handed him a crisp twenty from his leather wallet.

The man wrinkled his forehead and hesitated. "Tha old Madson place?"

Efram shrugged and took another guzzle from the bottle, watching as the young boy left the store and headed for the Porsche. "Whatever. I think it's the only house on the road. Least that's what my twit of a manager told me."

"Yeah, yeah, that's tha place." He reached under the counter. "Want a bag?"

Efram nodded. "Not too much farther, right?"

"You bought that house? You the artist?"

Efram tapped his foot. "I've already got a reputation?" This is what he had dreaded. He wanted to work without being disturbed. Besides, he had no interest in getting involved in the community. He didn't care about friendly neighbors. He just wanted to know how far away they were.

"People just curious," the man said and handed Efram his change. The dollar bills were wet; Efram quickly shoved them in his pocket, wondering whether the wetness was from gasoline or sweat.

"So it's close?" Efram glanced out the screen door and saw the boy sitting in the front seat, rubbing the steering wheel.

"Yeah, few mo' miles. Take a left ... "

Efram opened the screen door. "Look but don't touch, dammit!" he yelled. The boy jumped out and started to pet the dog. "He bites, by the way," Efram said. The boy jerked his hand away and walked around the car, observing every detail. Efram shut the door. "Sorry. So turn left, then?"

"Well, you'll be on Community Way, then left et tha college, right on Miller, left on Cedar. House et tha very end, only house."

"Great. Thanks." Efram picked up his snacks and went outside.

"Really, I didn't even say you could look, so you surely don't get in it!" Efram said to the boy, who was checking out the tires.

"Sorry. She's great. How does she run?"

"Is my car a girl?"

"Huh?"

"It runs fine. It's like sailing through Eden with speed, kid."

"Maybe I'll see ya in town?"

"Maybe. This place that small?"

The boy laughed. "Oh, yeah."

Efram got in his car. "So if I ran naked through the town square, everyone would know about it in a matter of minutes?"

"Yeah, but I wouldn't recommend it. They'd probably perform an exorcism, or something."

"No kiddin'? Well, there ain't nothing like a good cast-out-the-evil-spirits session to get a town jumping. At least they don't burn people at the stake. Those ropes would really chafe my skin." He said the last part with a Scarlett O'Hara accent. The boy grinned and went back inside. "Better keep me clothes on, Boogie, just in case."

The dog sniffed the sack. "Yeah, I got ya something. Quit your slobbering." He poured the last of the water from a thermos into a small orange bowl with the dog's name painted on the side. Around the bowl were little character sketches of Efram and the dog. Efram had designed it himself, which caused his one-time girlfriend and mentor, Alana Simpson, to roll her eyes.

"For a dog, Efram? That much trouble for a mutt!" she had said in her nasal, cocaine-inspired voice. Efram had created two more and sold them for five dollars, the price of the bowls, to a street vendor near Times Square. Hearing this, Alana rolled her blood-shot eyes again. "You're Efram T. Corbet. You can't go selling your stuff for pennies to street trash!"

"I thought you said they were stupid."

She had grunted and took another slurp of vodka. "Still got your name on them and your name's money."

"Didn't put my name on them."

Alana had slammed the glass down. "You're an idiot. You have no idea what this all means! Have you forgotten everything I taught you?"

Efram was trying to forget everything she had taught him. Her advice had led him into darkness. In the beginning he needed her. He was like a record, and she had control of the needle. With her assistance, Efram's voice was known to everyone in the art world. Over time, Efram realized that she had been scratching his record all along. His song was no longer clear.

After his parents died, Alana had tried to cheer him up by offering him a line of coke. Flipping over the table, the white powder soaring through the room, Efram had yelled like a beast, kicking Alana out of his life and himself into rehab. He had never touched drugs or alcohol again.

"Pepsi later. You need your water," Efram said after the dog lapped up the water. Efram revved up the engine and spun the car around, partly for show and mostly because he was tired and ready to check out his new place. Mr. Boogie flopped back against the seat when the car jerked into gear. "Sorry, 'bout that, fella." Annoyed, the dog jumped into the small back seat. "We'll be at our new home soon." Pulling onto the highway, Efram reached into the bag, opened the beef jerky with his teeth, and handed it to the dog.

Efram didn't bother putting up the top and turning on the air. He liked the way it made him look, driving with the top down, one hand casually slung over the wheel. Ever since he saw a Porsche at age ten in a friend's car magazine, he had wanted one. His father told him, "You'll need to paint a masterpiece to ever afford one of those." When Efram bought his first Porsche after his debut art showing, his father's only response was, "Gas guzzler. Don't know why you bought that thing."

Efram found the exit quickly. He drove through town, admiring the neatly lined-up houses. Almost every yard had a sprinkler on. He drove past the small community college and snorted. "People who can't go to real school." When he rolled into the town square, he bit his lip. "Oh gosh, I swear Andy and Barney are around here somewhere." Paint chipped off some of the buildings, but it was neat and clean. It took one stoplight to pass through the square, and when he reached Miller Road, Efram noticed that the houses were farther apart and most rested on large pieces of land. "This is cool."

He slowed down and shifted gears when he noticed that the road to his new home, Cedar Hill, wouldn't be smooth. "Gravel! What the hell? Marlon didn't video this part." After turning onto the road, he put the convertible in park and got out, the gravel scrunching under his feet. Putting his hand over his forehead, he looked down the road. Nothing, it seemed, but trees. He reached into the car and turned off the ignition. Walking in front of the car, he continued to look.

The screech of scratched metal made him turn around. "Mr. Boogie! Don't do that!" The dog was at Efram's feet, wagging his tail. His entire backside shook when he did this, as the tail was a curl flipped over like the letter C. Efram kneeled and patted the dog's head. "No more jumping out if you're going to scratch the sides. We've discussed this." He covered the dog's smashed, wrinkled face with his hand and rubbed his head back and forth. "Blah, your nose is wet." Mr. Boogie's tongue hung from his mouth and little drops of saliva landed on Efram's Gucci loafers, which were also covered in dust and little scuff marks. Efram rubbed the dog's head once more before Mr. Boogie ran into the woods. "Don't get lost, now," Efram hollered after him like a mother watching her son run off to play.

The sunlight reflected off the fender and temporarily blurred Efram's vision. Big spots of yellow and orange hovered in his line of sight. When his eyes stopped watering, he ran his hands over the sides of the car and thoroughly inspected the paint. He walked around the car, discovered that it was fine, and leaned against it, waiting for his dog to return.

Honeysuckle hugged an old fence that went up the road. Efram took a deep breath, enjoying the scent. He walked over to the vines and toyed with the flowers, tickling the buds lightly with his finger. Leaning over, he sniffed them. As a child he used to eat the flowers after biting off the ends and sucking out the nectar.

"You're not suppose to do that, stupid," his ten-year-old friend Curtis had told him. "Just suck the juice, you ma-ta-toe mulatto."

Irked, Efram had pulled off as much of the vine as he could and threatened his friend, "You want this upside your head?" He then proceeded to chase and swat Curtis until he was covered in welts. Curtis' mother had called to report the incident, and Efram ended up covered with blemishes from a switching. He had returned to the honeysuckle vines behind his house, crying and picking the flowers apart.

Efram's father, a heavyset house painter deeply scraped by scorn for marrying a black seamstress from Chicago, was never frugal when it came to the belt. Efram had it all memorized, the belt for bad grades and stupid mistakes, switches for misbehavior. The belt he hated, but he despised the marks the switches left on his legs for other children to see.

Usually, he only misbehaved when it came to art; his favorite game had involved splattering his father's cans of Sears All-Purpose on the ground to make "grass murals." Mrs. Corbet, a thin woman with a stripe of gray in her bunned hair, would critique Efram's work, then make him spray the yard clean before his father came home.

When his father was away on a job, his mother, if she didn't have a sewing engagement, would drive Efram to Memphis, a four-hour drive from Little Rock, to visit the art museum. She once told him that painting was like sewing, the needle being the eye to weave anything desired, just as the brush draws life into motion.

During one of his trips to the art museum, Efram saw the first painting he fell in love with, Maxfield Parrish's *Contentment*. He loved the colors, the scenery, and the beautiful women. He told his mother that someday he would buy it for her. He regretted never being able to do so.

His father only became interested in Efram's art after seeing the value of having a child graduate from college. At Mrs. Corbet's urging, Efram was allowed to take art classes at the YMCA, where his confidence grew.

As he did as a child, Efram pulled off one of the honeysuckle flowers and examined it, removing the stamen and biting off the end. The nectar mixed with a droplet of sweat that fell from his upper lip. He sucked out the juice just as Mr. Boogie came running back. Efram ignored him and put the flower in his mouth, letting it melt on his tongue before smoothing it against the roof of his mouth. The dog barked at his feet as Efram crushed the flower beneath his teeth. "Let's go, Boog. Let's see this place." Efram gave him a good-natured shove and the dog playfully growled back.

He filled Mr. Boogie's bowl with Pepsi and placed it on the dash. The dog lapped it up as Efram savored the honeysuckle on his breath. He smiled and started the car after taking a long swig of soda, enhancing the flower taste in his mouth. He put the dog's empty dish on the floor and started down the road, slowly. The gravel drive seemed like an eternity.

The bumps along the way made the dog knaw on the jerky as he jumped from front seat to back seat several times, snorting and sniffing, and driving Efram crazy. "Be still, dog. You can bury it later."

As much as Mr. Boogie wanted to bury his treat, Efram was just as anxious to see his new home. Efram would have purchased the house earlier, moving in on the same day, but his accountant had advised him to look at a few other places. When he caught glimpse of the house as he approached, Efram knew he had made the right decision.

A huge white house that looked like a mini-plantation with a wrap-around porch and stark white columns slowly revealed itself in the center of a yard surrounded by pine, willow, and magnolia trees. Flower gardens seemed to be everywhere. Several flowering vines slithered up the porch, embracing the house delicately like lace on a baby buggy. Pollen dusted the tranquil lake, waiting for something to make a ripple, like nature's powdered sugar. Two flower petals gently broke free from the breeze and floated down to the water.

He parked the car next to a tree stump. Smiling, he got out, staring with his mouth open. "Is this for real?" A huge willow tree swayed in the breeze, seeming to play chef by stirring the scents of the lake, the plants, the dirt, and the other trees. "Damn. This is great!" Rubbing his palms together, he giggled like a schoolboy.

Mr. Boogie put his paws on the dash. "Come on out, boy!" The dog jumped out and Efram made introductions: "Boogie, this is dirt. Dirt, Boogie. No more fire hydrants or cement for you, little dog." The dog panted, seeming to smile as Efram snapped his fingers. The dog took off, stopping occasionally to roll on the ground.

"Incredible!" Efram put his hands on his hips and walked over to the stump, stepping over tire tracks left by the moving vans. A root poked through the dirt and Efram tried to push it down with his toe. It would not sink into the dirt. He hopped on top of the stump and stood there with his legs firmly planted apart and declared, "Mine. All mine."

"Ouch!" Efram yelled as he stubbed his toe. He was still looking around for the best location for his white grand piano, the last detail in making the place look like home. During his first week in Wenton, he had moved the instrument from place to place in the living room. "I guess over by this window will work. It's close to my work area, but not so close I'll get paint on it." Efram nodded. "Yep. That's it." He pushed the piano, his bare, sweaty feet sliding on the hardwood floor.

After positioning the instrument, he put his hands on his hips and looked around the room. He was quite happy with his new surroundings; he even liked the click of his heels on the hardwood floors, but what he liked most was the way the sunlight slid in through the windows, hit the floor, and rebounded to the walls and ceiling. During the day, light filled the house like the soft light in a studio portrait – perfect for him to work. At night, the house darkened like a stage after a show. The atmosphere inspired him. Each night before bed, when he had free time and wasn't too tired from moving furniture, he sketched the house, the flowers, the lake, and anything else he found charming.

Now that everything was in place, he could finally turn his attention fully to his art. He fixed a glass of iced herbal tea, patted Mr. Boogie, and went out on the porch to absorb the humidity and smell the blooms. He sat in the porch swing, sipping his tea with a lemon half dangling for life on the side, and did nothing, except think. Slowly, after he felt inspired, he moved to the living room, where his easel was standing, and tried to paint, but his paintbrush said nothing. He scratched his neck and stared at the canvas. "Okay, this isn't good. Better go outside and have a talk with the bushes and trees for inspiration. Come on, Boog, let's go out." The dog, curled into a ball on the couch, refused Efram's efforts to get him into the sun. Efram put on his sandals. "All right, stay inside with the air conditioner. See if I care." He lightly slapped the dog's behind.

Stepping once again into the hot sun, Efram wondered why his talent was escaping him. He was alone, he had peace and quiet, and the phone didn't interrupt his concentration. Stepping off the porch, he walked towards the woods. A bluebird frolicking in the cement bath chirped at him, but when he walked over to the bird, it quickly flew away. Efram looked at his reflection in the water. The tall pine trees loomed behind him. "I wonder what's out there?"

Vines stuck to his jeans and dirt dusted his toes as he strolled, remembering walks like this as a child. The woods had been his favorite place to hide then, providing cover, solitude, and inspiration. He would often carry his notebook paper and crayons, which he first dutifully sharpened at the picnic table, and head for the woods behind his house. Sometimes he'd climb up in a tree and color the grass below him. "Gotta get up high to see all the color," he told himself. After a long day of coloring, he would bring the drawings to his mother so she could tack them on the refrigerator. She called it Efram's "art gallery," which always made him proud. He would saunter off and tell her to expect more drawings the next day.

Efram started to climb a tree, but his sandals slipped on the bark. He jumped up to catch the branch above him, but missed. Leaning against the tree, he laughed. "Somewhere along the way, I've lost my childhood abilities." He thought for a moment, then leaned his head all the way back to look at the tops of the pines. They seemed to meet at the top and encompass Efram, protecting him. After watching the trees sway in the slight breeze that moderately cooled the air, he went inside to splatter his emotions in watercolor, a medium he hadn't used since childhood.

Chapter 5

Cupid's Dart

Joy arrived home, after wandering around town to collect her thoughts. Her heart was still fluttering like a hummingbird's wings. Carelessly, she threw her book bag on the sofa, barely missing Katie who sat with the phone attached to her left ear.

Katie rolled her eyes. "Where you been? You gonna help me make dinner?" she called as Joy walked towards the kitchen.

Joy got herself a Dr Pepper and took a long drink before plopping down at the bar. Swiveling on the tan vinyl bar stool, she let out a long sigh and looked over the paper, which had been thoughtlessly thrown in the bushes by an over-eager, underpaid paper boy. As she flipped to the entertainment section, the whir of an engine outside startled her.

"Whoa! Sweet ride!" Katie yelled from the living room. She skipped to the kitchen and took a seat at the table. "Somebody in town has a very nice car! I swear it was a Porsche. I bet it was that rich artist guy who Mom sold that house to."

"Oh, really," Joy said, feigning interest in the paper.

"Braves win?" Katie asked.

"Uh, don't know." Joy found the sports section and handed it to her sister. "You cookin' dinner?"

"How 'bout we let Emily do it."

Joy smiled. "Good idea."

Emily arrived home ten minutes later, bursting with gossip. After she threw her purse on the table, she said, "Well, that artist guy made his first major public appearance. You know, the guy who bought the Madson home? He stopped by Brooke's Grocery, and ... you're not going to believe this!"

Joy slid off her seat and opened the refrigerator door, pretending to search for another soft drink.

"What? Enough with the dramatic pauses," Katie said, twisting her hair.

"He marched right in there and asked where he could buy fresh flowers. Mr. Brooke wondered why he'd want fresh flowers when he has a whole slew of them around his estate, but mentioned the florist on Vine anyway. Then, this guy named off a bunch of exotic ones and ol' man Brooke didn't have a clue. So, this guy wanted to know where the nearest health food store was. Girls ... the man *eats* flowers!"

"Well, with the garden Mrs. Madson left behind, he should be set for life," Katie said dryly. "Amazing how those flowers kept blooming after she died."

"He also bought watercolors," Joy said, taking her seat again.

The room went quiet for a second.

"How do you know?" Katie asked.

Joy crinkled her nose, reached over, and bopped Katie on the head. "I was there."

"Oh my gosh! Joy!" Emily said and grabbed Joy's wrists. "So, what'd he look like? Everyone said he was real trendy-like."

"He seemed fine." Joy shook off Emily's grip and got up to leave.

"That's it? Give us the scoop, already!" Katie said, pulling Joy's arm.

"There's nothing to tell." Joy started to walk out of the kitchen, only to run into her mother.

"Tell what?" Beverly asked and kissed Joy on the head.

Emily and Katie smiled. "Joy saw that guy. That guy who bought the Madson place," Katie told her.

"Efram Corbet?"

"Does he drive a Porsche?" Katie wanted to know, still fantasizing about the car. "I want a ride in that car!"

"Yes, I saw him, okay! And yes he drives a Porsche!" Joy

yelled, waving her arms. "Big deal. Can I leave now?" She put her hands on her hips.

"What, no details?" Beverly asked.

"No details. Ask them," Joy said and left to go to her room.

"I bet he's gay," Katie said, shoveling grapes into her mouth like a backhoe.

Joy heard the comment and came back into the kitchen. "Oh, you're so stupid. You think everyone's gay, especially if they don't have grease under their nails, or ... if they have an IQ."

"Whatever!" Katie said, sucking the pulp out of a grape.

"Girls, hush. I have a headache," Beverly said, stroking Joy's brown hair. Joy flipped it back and pushed it behind her ear. "You have homework, Joy?"

"Yes," Joy said and left the kitchen again.

In her room, she sprawled out on her stomach on the bed. She had seen Efram Corbet earlier in the day and couldn't seem to get him out of her mind. As on any other day, she stopped by Brooke's Grocery, which doubled as a soda fountain, for a cherry coke, a cheeseburger, and a little eavesdropping on the "checker club," a group of elderly men who spent the day drinking coffee and playing checkers. They swapped stories with the working class who came by for burgers or chicken-fried steak. Joy knew all the older gentlemen who hung out in the store. They would kid her about her "wacky" dreams of moving to another country to search for lost treasure. "Indiana Jones, huh? Gonna find the golden monkey?" they would tease and she would politely grin.

Joy ventured down to Brooke's after her class let out early and took a seat at the lunch counter. She secured her rear-end carefully on the cool vinyl, half-expecting a hot seat from the smoldering sun outside, and ordered a cherry Coke. Brushing the sweaty strands of hair out of her face, she glanced around the room which carried the smell of cigars, churned ice cream, and bags of flour. The store's blue wallpaper peeled at the edges, partly from its fifty-year existence and possibly from the hair-raising tales that its many patrons told. The white, gold-speckled Formica tables were perfect for a heated checkers game, lunch, or a gossip party of four. The blue chairs and bar stools, though not so comfortable, welcomed guests to stay and have a chocolate malt.

As generations had stopped by to pick up groceries and chit-chat, the hardwood floors showed their age with scrape marks. However, they were never dusty or dirty. The shine lingered from the heavy wax that Mr. Brooke plastered on them each night after closing shop at six o'clock. He had found that the mall a few miles away took his business after working hours. The young kids almost never came by, preferring McDonald's for a Big Mac. Joy was the exception, since she didn't have a car and the store was close to college.

"The usual, Miss Baxter?" Mr. Brooke asked, pulling a plastic cup from under the counter.

"Yep. Cherry Coke, double cheeseburger, fries. Thanks." Joy swiveled on her bar stool and looked at the old-fashioned Coke and Pepsi signs above the soda fountain. "That guy from Coke ever call again?"

Before removing a hamburger patty from the freezer and dropping it on the grill with the rest of the sizzling burgers, Mr. Brooke fixed Joy's drink, using a hefty amount of cherry grenadine. "Naw. Reckon he was pullin' my chain. He didn't want to buy that sign a'tall."

"Maybe he found a cheaper one at a flea market or somethin'."

Mr. Brooke ignored her and kept on flipping patties like a well-trained fry cook. Joy turned her attention to a little boy, almost school age, who tugged at his mother's skirt begging for a cardboard airplane that required "some assembly" of putting tab A in slot B. The "general store" was on the right with five aisles of groceries, school supplies, toiletries and other necessities; the back section was refrigerated, with soft drinks, dairy products, and beer. The kid got his way, and Joy smiled while she sipped her Coke. As she crunched on the ice, she reached for her oversized geology book that barely fit into her leather book bag. Quietly soaking up the down-home atmosphere, she read chapter three about the earth's layers.

Occasionally, she glanced up from her book, amused by the old men caught up in their heated checker game. Eventually, engrossed in her studies and her cheeseburger, she lost track of who was whipping whose butt in checkers and failed to hear the tinkling of the little bell above the door. The spring door clanged shut after the customer and Joy could feel it catching the person's heel. The loud chatting and laughter ceased and whispers encompassed the room. Joy first assumed it was the town harlot stopping by to pick up liquor for a male suitor. Then the odor of cologne swept by her and she wondered who had such a wonderful aroma; most men in town were farmers or carpenters and smelled of the earth. After she heard enough snickers, she turned around. Behind one of the aisles she saw an unfamiliar head bobbing up and down to a rhythm that must have been internal. The head disappeared behind the school-supplies section, and then, with a two-dollar plastic container of watercolors, the stranger sauntered up to the counter, coming into view like a painting coming into perspective.

Efram Corbet, the most gorgeous man Joy Baxter had ever seen, stood only three feet away from her to pay for his art supplies. All the men in town looked almost the same, blue collar, but this guy did not have harsh, sunburned skin or oil stains on his jeans. The only thing he had in common with them was his T-shirt, which had spots of paint at the bottom. The shirt was cut off at the shoulders and revealed his toned arms. Tight black jeans hugged his legs. His feet, in black suede boots, hardly made a sound when he had strolled down the hardwood floor. Not much taller than 5'9, he walked like a king, head held high, seemingly oblivious to the men's chuckling on his behalf. Joy rather admired the way he ignored the men.

Efram reached into his back pocket to remove his wallet. He placed it on the counter, then took off his sunglasses, revealing curious, onyx eyes. A strand of hair came loose from his ponytail and trickled over his honey-colored skin.

Suddenly aware that her mouth literally hung open, Joy shut it and bit her lip. Efram shot her a look that wasn't necessarily friendly, or unfriendly, for that matter. It was just a look. She quickly turned away, as most people do when they get caught staring.

"That be all?" Mr. Brooke asked.

Efram tapped his fingers on the counter. "Where can I buy flowers?" He glanced at Joy. She kept her face in her book, turning the pages slowly and only looking at Efram from the corners of her eyes.

"We have seeds. What kind ya lookin' for?" Mr. Brooke replied, noticing that Efram's full attention had turned to Joy. "Sir?"

"Nasturtiums?"

Mr. Brooke shook his head.

"Day lilies? Surely there is a place where I can get day lilies? Do they grow anywhere around the fields or roads around here? I want them for a salad."

Mr. Brooke was silent for a minute, then suggested a nearby flower shop. Efram thanked him, looked at Joy once more, and paid for his watercolors. Turning on his heel, and placing his glasses over his eyes, Efram Corbet left the store. Joy twisted around on the bar stool to watch him leave.

"Wasn't that something," remarked one of the locals. Joy gathered her books, hopped off the stool, and ran out the door into the eyes of a pug panting in the sun. The dog's head hung over the door of a black convertible. It seemed to be wearing a huge smile instead of trying to overcome the heat.

Efram opened the car door and got in, while Joy pretended to rifle through her book bag. He patted the dog, then clutched the steering wheel, watching Joy try not to stare. Back and forth, up and down, Efram squeezed the wheel's leather band, while taking in Joy's presence. Behind her, he could see several old eyes peeking through the store window.

I should start charging admission, he thought.

Then Joy swung her hair out of her face and his attention went back to her. He lifted up, leaned over the steering wheel, and placed his folded arms on top of the windshield. He unraveled a sneaky grin that took up his entire face like the Cheshire cat in *Alice in Wonderland*. Taking a deep breath, he said, "Hi."

Joy immediately stopped searching for an item that wasn't lost and let her eyes look from side to side without peering up. Efram slid back down in his seat and she nodded. He snuggled himself in the seat, all the while with the same grin on his lips. He started the car; the stereo blared *I Second That Emotion*. Joy's ears perked up like a puppy's at play.

"Come on, Mr. Boogie," Efram said.

Joy watched him peel away and reached her hand behind her neck, wrenching it like a workman might do after being in the sun all day. She smiled to herself, letting out a nervous chuckle.

Joy wandered around town for about an hour, Efram's face lingering in her memory like a sweet piece of candy. Like any good treat, it left a desire for more. She walked down Miller Road, passing her home and wondering if he'd renamed the Madson house the Corbet Estate and put a sign at the end of the gravel driveway. That was a good enough excuse to keep walking. When she got to the end of the sidewalk, she stopped. The gravel drive swept down towards the Madson house. She rocked back and forth on the cement, her toes hanging off the crumbling edge. The cracks in the sidewalk split two ways, and one, she thought, resembled Efram's wicked grin. With her foot, she pushed a tiny pebble into the crack and lightly nudged it. It would not budge from its new home. As the wind blew, the dust nipped at her ankles and rose up to hit her face. A few loose sprinkles got in her eye, and she grabbed her eyelid, letting the tears wash away the dust. She reached into her book bag, pulled out a Kleenex, and wiped her eye. Then she stepped off the sidewalk onto the driveway. The sand and gravel crunched under her weight and made its way into the crevices of her sole.

As she cautiously strolled, not knowing what to expect, especially if he should see her, the trees began to thicken. She started to smell the lake, and in her mind, she could hear children splashing and Mr. Madson yelling "Dog paddle! Dog paddle!" That was the only way Katie could swim after falling in the frozen lake at age seven, thinking the sheet of ice would be thick enough for ice skating. Mr. Madson had hollered the swimming technique to her as he ran to rescue her that day. As the familiar sounds, smells, and sights hovered around her, the sound of an unfamiliar dog yapping crept up on her. Then, as the house came into view, she saw the black convertible parked casually by a tree stump, as if it had always belonged there.

She stepped off the road and into the woods. Immediately, she found the old trails she had followed as a child. One led all the way back to her own house. From many days spent playing cops and robbers, she knew the trails were not only a means of getting from point A to point B; they also offered camouflage.

She tried not to crunch too many leaves or rustle too many branches as she crouched in the brush, praying that he was somewhere outside so she could get another look at him. The dog was no longer barking and music drifted into her ears. It was a piano, playing *This Magic Moment*.

"This guy really has great taste in music," she said to herself.

Her curiosity beat fear into the ground, and she decided to go in for a closer look.

"Careful," she whispered, feeling like a robber again. "Don't make a sound. Stay low." She imagined a childhood friend hiding behind Efram's car waiting to throw her in pretend-jail.

When she reached the house, Joy paused briefly to admire a bed of cupid's darts that grew by the porch. Then she climbed on the porch and slipped through the rails. Like a spy in a television action drama, she flattened her back against the wall and slowly edged her way to the open windows where the breeze blew the sheer white curtains up. Peering in, she saw Efram playing the piano. The curtain flicked and tapped her face, disturbing her snooping. Seeing that the door was also open, she cautiously moved towards it, put her hand on the frame, and peaked around it. It was a romantic setting. Efram, now wearing a white silk shirt over his T-shirt, sat at the piano. The breeze from outside, and the ceiling fan, billowed the sleeves of his shirt, making him look almost angelic. Lightly, he sang the words to the song. He played like a man making love, making the instrument sing like any canvas he had ever applied color to. She smiled. He was beautiful to her.

Peering into his private world, she felt guitly, but was unable to turn away. Joy was totally lost in the moment and didn't notice the smiling face at her feet until the pug panted and slobbered on her leg. Joy jumped back and swallowed. The dog was still indoors and had only put its head out to look at her. Any moment, she knew, it would let out a playful bark. She leaned back against the wall, trying to press herself as flat as the paint covering it. The dog leaned around to find her and barked. Efram stopped playing. Joy balled up her fists and bit her lip. "Just be calm," she whispered.

"Boogie?" Efram turned to see the dog staring out the door. Seeing nothing else, he turned back and continued to peck at the keys. Fearing she would get caught, Joy started to bolt, but then she heard Efram begin the first lines to *My Girl*. She tried to discourage the pug by gently pushing at it with her toe, but the dog took it as an invitation to play and started growling and tugging at her sandal. Thinking fast, Joy broke a twig from a rose bush and hurled it into the yard. The dog darted out the doorway and leaped off the porch.

From the corner of his eye, Efram saw the twig fly across his porch and his pet run after it. "Boog?" he said as he got up to investigate. Mr. Boogie ran back up the steps after retrieving the twig, and Joy, not knowing what else to do, threw it again. Startled, Efram ran to the door. Joy bit her lip and crouched down, trying to hide, but she could feel Efram's eyes on her back. He grabbed her arm and yanked her up. His eyes were slits.

"You want ... ," Efram hesitated and loosened his grip when he saw Joy's face. "You want something?"

"Oh, sorry, no more Girl Scout cookies!" she blurted and jerked her arm from his grip. His eyes widened. They stared at each other, then she ran, faster than a bumblebee's flight, careful not to trample the cupid's darts. Into the woods she went, as Efram watched her, shaking his head.

Mr. Boogie sat at Efram's feet, twig in his mouth. "Who was that, Boog?" Efram took the twig and patted the dog's head. "Strange girl."

Honeysuckle, he thought, as he went back inside and sat on the couch. The girl smelled like honeysuckle. Either that, or all the flowers around his house were starting to damage his sense of smell.

"What do you think, Boog?" he asked the pug, who was now curled up at his feet. "She's a lil' pixie of a thing. Pretty cute." The dog snorted and crawled closer to Efram's leg. "Oh, what would you know? You're a dog. A neutered dog, for that matter, so your opinion doesn't count!" He ruffled the dog's short hair. "Maybe the town spy will pay us another visit."

Chapter 6

Lavender

The dark puff-ball cloud held its ground above Efram's car. The rain pounded on the windshield and nearly blurred his vision. The storm rumbled and shot out lines of lightning.

"I can't believe this damn thing is leaking," Efram said, glancing up at the tiny drops of water falling from the roof and landing on the seats. He poked at the convertible's top and felt for holes. "Really sucks."

As he rounded a corner, he saw someone walking along in the downpour. "Now that's a stupid person, Boog. You think we should slow down or splash them?" The dog lifted its head and barked. "What? Boogie, how rude! We can't do ... " Efram slowed down. "Boog, well, what do we have here? It's our friendly, neighborhood Girl Scout." He nudged the dog. "Hop in the back, Mr. Boog. Let's give her a ride. I have a hankering for some cookies." The dog barked. "Get in the back!" Efram pushed the dog until it obeyed.

Joy turned her head as the car drove alongside her. Her red-and-white flowered sundress held on to her like static cling. The car's headlights illuminated her shadow. She kept her head down. Of all the cars to pass beside her it had to be him.

Efram rolled down the window. "Would you like a ride?" he asked. She shook her head and kept walking. "Hey, I understand," he said, driving with one arm slung over the steering wheel. "But it's coming down pretty hard. Besides, could a man with a pug be dangerous?" He offered a friendly smile and stopped the car. He reached over to the door handle and tried to push it open. "Sticks sometimes. As much as I paid, you'd think it'd open at my command."

Joy stood there staring at him. The rain poured down her face and she could barely see.

"Come on. Where do you live?" he asked.

She swallowed and climbed into the car. "Thank you," she whispered. "402 Miller. Miller Road."

Efram looked at her soaked body. "I don't think the U.S. swim team has ever been as drenched as you are right now. I'm Efram, Efram Corbet." He extended his hand. "I believe you've already met my dog, Mr. Boogie."

She shook his hand and grinned. "Joy Baxter."

"Hi, Joy. Lovely name." He looked at the book bag she held in her lap. "So, what do ya have in the bag? Cookies?"

"Cookies? Uh ... oh ... no. Books. I go to the college." She swept the wet hair behind her ears, then wiped her face on her arm.

"Oh, sorry," he said and opened the glove compartment. "Here's some tissues. A car's not complete without Kleenex and moist towelettes." She rubbed the tissues over her face. "So, where's your badge?" he asked.

"Badge?"

"Your badge that certifies you as the new-guy-in-town inspector."

Joy shook her head. "Sorry."

"What's with the curiousity anyway? I'm not a sadist with a harem of love slaves or anything. Although I once knew a man with three wives. Sick, really."

After wiping her face and arms, Joy balled up the tissues. She had no excuse for being at his house, no ready-made lie. "I was out walking. Your house is sort of behind mine, behind the woods. There're trails. That's all ... just wandered too far."

"So far that you landed on my doorstep?"

She touched her upper lip with the tip of her tongue and looked down. His hand rested on the gear shift, barely touching it, only clutching it when he needed to. Little drops of water landed on his fingers. Joy looked up and saw the drops weren't from her but from the dripping ceiling.

Noticing her glance up, he said, "Don't know why it's leaking. Can't feel the holes."

She smiled at him and looked away. "You're almost there."

"Huh?" he asked and saw 402 Miller written in black stencil near the door of a white clapboard house. "That your house?"

"Yes. Go 'round back."

Efram pulled into the driveway and parked under the rusted carport. "You don't drive? Or you like to stroll in the rain?"

"No car." She tried to open the door, but it stuck again.

"Here." Efram reached over her rain-soaked body and pulled the handle. "Hmm. Can't get the thing," he said. She leaned back into her seat. The smell of his cologne, lavender, hovered under her nose. Lavender is suppose to have calming properties, Joy thought, but *his* smell only made her more excited. Efram pushed on the door until it popped open. Joy smiled politely, hoping he couldn't read her mind, which was filled with thoughts of his hair between her fingers. When Efram sat back up, his hair lightly grazed her face, causing her to shiver. "Cold?" he asked. "You better get in and get warmed up."

"Thank you. Bye," Joy said and stepped into the thrashing rain.

"Sure," he said and watched her run towards the three porch steps. Her skirt had made itself a second skin and clearly defined Joy's slender legs. "Hey!" he opened the car door and shouted. Joy turned, pulled the hair from her face, and squinted. "Those woods go to my house?" Efram asked.

She nodded, waved, and ran inside. Efram sat there for a few moments watching the rain hit the hood of the car. Mr. Boogie jumped into the front seat. "Whoa! You scared me, Boog." Glancing down, Efram noticed Joy's maroon fake-leather purse on the floor. He picked it up and dashed through the rain to her door.

In a state of undress, Joy quickly threw on her robe and ran to answer the knock. "Why the hell isn't anyone else home? I have to do everything," she muttered on the way to the back door. Upon opening it, she saw Efram standing there and gasped. "Yes?" she asked, pulling her robe together.

"You forgot your purse." He held it out to her.

She tugged on the terry-cloth belt around her waist. "Thanks."

"Sure," he answered. The little canopy above the steps wasn't much protection from the downpour, so he waved and ran back to the car. Joy tilted her head, admiring him. He clapped his hands together as if he was playfully trying to smash the raindrops. She could hear him humming as he opened the car door. The little dog inside barked, obviously ready to go home.

Chapter 7

Day Lilies

Joy skipped most of the way to Efram's house. In addition to the prospect of seeing Efram, it was Friday, she had minimal homework for the weekend, only one chapter to read in geology, and forty dollors left in her weekly self-allowance, which meant she could do a little shopping. She lightly jiggled the bag of Chips Ahoy cookies, being careful not to break them. Even if it created another humiliating encounter, the cookies were intended as a peace offering, to make a fresh start. Still moderately intimidated from her previous actions and encounters with him, she had to remind herself that Efram had seemed like a fun, nice guy. The fact that he was incredibly sexy also gave her more moxy to get to know him better.

Mr. Boogie ran to greet her when she stepped into Efram's yard. He wagged his curled tail and panted wildly. "I think he likes me," Joy said to herself. "Is your master home?" The dog ran in circles, and Joy picked up a stick and threw it. He ran after it while she headed for the house.

She knocked on the open door. Peering inside, she saw no one. Humming came from the kitchen, then the clatter of dishes and a loud smack. "Die, Nazi bug, die!" Efram yelled. A whack. Then a thud. "Ha! Thought you could outrun me! Well, you were *wrong*!"

"Mental note. He's scared of bugs." Joy laughed and stepped

into the doorway. "Anybody home?"

Efram came into the living room holding a rolled-up newspaper. When he saw Joy, he jumped back, not expecting anyone to be at his door. The newspaper fell from his hand and a large, black water bug slipped off its murderer.

"Sorry," Joy said. "Didn't mean to scare you."

Efram frowned and picked up the paper, carefully scooping up the bug without touching it. "You have a bad habit of nosing around." He walked past her and flicked the bug into the yard.

"I'm not nosing around. I brought you a thank-you gift ... for picking me up in the rain." She handed him the cookies. "It's a name brand. We were all sold out down at Scout headquarters." She put her hands behind her back and rocked on her heels.

Efram put the newspaper under his arm and took the cookies, shaking his head. "Scout headquarters, right. Girl, you're wacky."

"Well, actually, I brought you the cookies so you'd think I *wasn't* wacky."

"Hmm," Efram said. "Isn't it weird how our intentions never turn out the way we plan?" He opened the bag and bit into a cookie. "But you're in luck. I like wacky."

"Whew," Joy said and wiped her hand across her forehead.

"It was right neighborly of you, though. I really did move to Mayberry, didn't I?" he asked, leaning against the doorway and pointing the cookie at her.

"No. I'd bring you a freshly baked, homemade, triple-layer, chocolate cake if it was Mayberry."

Efram put the rest of the cookie into his mouth. "Very true." He swallowed and nodded. "Well, thanks anyway."

"What's that coming from the kitchen?" Joy asked.

"What? What's coming from the kitchen? Another one of those damn bugs?" Efram raised the newspaper.

Joy wrinkled her nose. "Uh, no, the smell. What're you cooking?"

"Oh. Don't scare me like that," he said and bopped her on the head with the paper. "I'm making lunch. Hungry?"

"Smells wonderful," she said, following him into the kitchen.

It was strange for her to walk through the house that had once been so familiar. The interior was now more modern, no real sense of anyone or anything old ever having been there. A sleek, black leather couch, two metallic-looking end tables, and a massive entertainment system completed the furniture in the sparse room. It was decorated with paintings and plants. A large unpainted canvas, surrounded by cans of Dutch Boy paint, leaned against the piano. "What're you gonna paint?" she asked.

"What am I going to paint?" He paused. "I don't know yet."

"It's a really big canvas."

"I have really big ideas." As he entered the kitchen and threw the cookies and paper on the counter, he mimicked a French accent. "One does not merely paint. One must let inspiration touch him. It just comes." He clasped his hands against his chest. "I am merely a medium. I do not yet know what it will say." He thumped a salad bowl like it was a ripe watermelon. "Om."

"And I'm the wacky one." Joy sat down at the table.

Efram laughed. "I don't take myself that seriously."

"An artist who doesn't take himself seriously. Film at eleven."

"No sense stressing too much. Life is strange, surreal, fun. That doesn't mean I don't take my work seriously. I do. Very much so."

He pulled out two plates, two bowls, and two forks and stacked them on the table before continuing. "I love painting, but if I let myself take it too seriously, I start to believe I am great and powerful. Success can do that to you." He lifted the lid from the wok. Steam was seeping out the edges, and he was careful not to burn himself. Joy could smell the sweet chicken and vegetables simmering. Efram shook the wok then stirred the food. The smell was taking over the room like flowers in spring. "I'm not near as arrogant as people claim."

Joy lifted her eyebrows. "You don't say."

"I do say." Efram sat down across from her.

"So what's the scoop on you anyway?"

"The scoop? Ah, yes, the scoop. I'm only part black for the nosy people in town who want to know. My father was white, so maybe that'll alleviate some of their fears."

"Um, no, I wanted to know if you're really famous?" Joy asked and played with a flower petal that had fallen from a vase in the center of the table.

He stood up to stir the concoction in the wok again. "Oh. Well, you could say that. As someone so bluntly pointed out, I'm not exactly Michael Jackson, but I have been known to draw a crowd now and then."

"Cool."

"Sometimes it's cool. Sometimes it's not."

They were silent for a few minutes. Joy toyed with the edges of a place mat. "Not everyone in town is a bigot, you know," she said. "You think because it's the South ... "

Efram stopped stirring and nodded. "I'm from Arkansas."

"Get out! Really?"

"Born and raised." Removing the vase, then placing a bowl of salad on the table, he snatched the place mat from under Joy's hand. "I will not wash place mats," he said.

"Then why are they here? Aren't they suppose to catch the spilled food?"

"No, a mere decoration. That's what my mother said." In a neat pile, he placed them on the counter.

"Anal," Joy remarked.

He pinched two fingers together. "Just a tad."

"I thought artists weren't supposed to be anal. They have to be spontaneous, creative ... "

"Organization and neatness don't deny creativity, Joy." He dumped the contents of the wok into a large glass bowl, then opened the refrigerator door and pulled out a glass pitcher of ice water. The sides were almost frosted, and Joy noticed the steam rising from the top as Efram placed it beside the hot food. "Lime?" he asked as he poured water into two glasses, giving Joy the one with a flower painted on the side.

"No, thanks. I've never cared much for lime or lemon in my water." Joy studied the glass. "Interesting. Did you paint the flower on this?"

He smiled. "Yes. Nice of you to notice."

Joy leaned over to sniff the chicken stir-fry. He dished out a heaping portion, along with salad. Joy poked around in her salad before tasting it and noticed it had day lilies in it. "Aren't flowers poisonous?"

she asked.

"If so, we're both doomed." Efram took a bite, grabbed his throat, and gagged.

Joy sucked her tooth. "Amusing."

"Don't you people around here like jokes?"

"Funny ones," Joy said dryly.

Efram tilted his head. "You don't think my jokes are funny?"

"Have I heard one?"

Efram slapped the table. "Ha! I guess you haven't then! Trust me. I'm hilarious."

Joy shook her head and started eating. "You're a weird guy."

"Probably what everybody around here thinks." Efram said with his mouth full.

"Maybe. They're just curious. Just don't destroy the moral fiber of the community and you'll do all right."

"That was my evil plan. Damn. Now I have to find another one."

She laughed and bit into the salad. Against her mouth, she felt a petal and enjoyed the sweet sensation. "This is really good. You're a great cook."

"Thanks." Efram took a few more bites of salad, savoring the Caesar dressing.

"So, about this fame thing ... "

"What about it?"

"Hey, I've never met anyone famous before, okay!"

Efram leaned over. "I was in *People* magazine once. Not to mention *Time* and *Life*. Don't make me pull them out." He shook his finger at her and Joy laughed.

"My mom sold you the house, but she didn't get much gossip from your agent."

"No kidding! Small town, for sure! If your mom knew the real me, my life history, she might not let me live here! Moral decay rampant."

She watched him dig into the stir-fry. He chewed very slowly, savoring each bite, and she imagined that was the way he enjoyed life, too. With his finger, he pulled out a petal and let it rest on his tongue, almost as if he was letting it melt. Joy let her eyes roam around the kitchen, enjoying the sight of it the same way he took in the food. It was a moment before she realized it used to be the Madson's kitchen. The old white Kenmore stove and refrigerator had been replaced by silver appliances. The magnets were gone, as were the gold-metal, chicken decorations on the walls. Instead, Efram had hung, on the wall opposite the stove, his painting called *Mine*. The only thing familiar that still remained was a burnt ring on the white counter top near the stove where Mrs. Madson had left a hot pot for too long. Efram had chosen a sheer material, similar to what he had in the living room, to replace the daisy curtains. It was still neat, however, and Joy knew Mrs. Madson would have approved of any kitchen that was in order.

"Did you paint that?" Joy asked.

Efram glanced up. "Yup." He told her the name of the portrait, then added, "And, this house is, well, mine."

Joy squirmed in her seat. "So, Efram, I once took an art appreciation class, and I was wondering what kind of stuff you paint. I mean, what's it called?" She pushed her fork back and forth along her plate.

"Ah, art appreciation! I bet you learned sooo much." He rolled his eyes.

"Well, I rather liked it. But I'm not an art major."

"One doesn't major in art. One lives it," he remarked, clenching his fist next to his chest.

"Oh boy, here comes the clenched-fist artist crap again."

Efram frowned. "No. I'm serious this time. Let me ask you this. Did they teach you about passion? Or did you simply memorize painting titles?"

"I got a good understanding of some basic knowledge."

"To fully appreciate great art, you have to know about the passion behind it."

"I want to be an archeologist or paleontologist. The art history class ... it was no big deal." She got up to put her salad bowl in the sink. He leaned back in his chair, watching her scrape the remains of her salad into the trash compactor. She pulled out a missed petal, ate it, then sat back down without turning on the trash compactor.

"I paint life. Beautiful women. Passion. Potential. Dreams.

Whatever I see that's real. Uncover the truth. It's usually so obvious, but people ignore the simple truths in front of them."

Joy felt a twinge of jealousy at the beautiful women comment. To stifle her jealous tendency, she started on the stir-fry. "This is better than the take-out place here," she told him.

"Of course. Learned from Julia Child."

Joy swallowed. "Really?"

With his mouth full, Efram replied, "No, made that up." He swallowed his food. "So what's the scoop on you? How old are you anyway?"

"Me? I'm twenty. Don't you know you're not suppose to ask a woman her age?"

"I have no manners. That happens when you pass thirty."

"Old man."

"Not too old. Just thirty-two."

"Old."

"Relative." He grinned. "Besides, I'm a lot smarter now than I was at twenty. A decade from now you'll agree."

"Maybe. Right now, I want to finish up my studies here at the community college. I'll be done in December, then I'll head to a university and get my degree in archeology."

"You like digging up things?"

"I like discovering treasure."

"Then we aren't too different."

Joy smiled.

When they were both finished eating, Efram stared at her for a moment, then said, "Come on, I want to show you something." He got up, took her hand, and led her to the back porch where his easel was set up with a half-finished piece of work on it. It was a watercolor painting of the woods and lake. Beside the painting was a white stool and art supplies. She could envision him sitting there, the sun coming down, working on some masterpiece, if he created masterpieces.

"What do you think?" he asked, holding it up for her.

Joy put her hand to her chest. "You want my college-art-class opinion?"

"Normally, I don't give a damn about anyone's opinion. If

someone gets it, that's great. If they don't, too bad for them. Besides, you aren't an art buyer with dollar signs floating in your eyes, so I'm curious how you feel. You know, from one treasure hunter to another." Efram sat down on the stool and put the painting in front of his legs.

"Well, it looks lovely."

Efram frowned. "Lovely?"

"All right, it's ugly."

"Hmm. Could be. Not all paintings are meant to hang in the doctor's office. What do you see?"

"Peace. I use to come here often as a child." Joy pointed to the lake. "We played in that lake. Brings back memories." She hesitated for a moment. "But that isn't what you were thinking when you painted it."

"Doesn't matter. I captured the peacefulness of this place."

She reached out to stroke it, then remembered what her teacher said about never touching paintings. "The water is moving. I can see it flowing. The ripples are subtle like always. I can almost hear it, but you know, I'd add more movement to the willows." She bit her lip and looked at him uncertainly.

"That's okay. I once told a teacher that the Sistine Chapel could've been better! I was a cocky kid."

"Was?"

"I rather like my arrogance," he said as he got up, smiling. Walking over to the door, he pointed inside. "You know that large canvas in there?" Joy nodded. "Well, I have this weird feeling that something soon will overwhelm me and I'll need that. Don't know what yet, but it'll surface soon. I love a blank canvas. So many possibilities!" He walked up to Joy. "Kinda like life."

Joy smiled. "If it has passion."

Efram came close to her. "Exactly." He stared into her eyes and reached to put his hands on her face.

Joy looked down and stepped back. "I really should be going," she replied and started to go inside.

He put his hand on her shoulder. "I'm sorry. Stay."

"Uh, no, can't. School. Homework. Test Tuesday." She walked into the house and headed for the front door. She stopped as if she had come to the ledge of a tall building. The praying hands were no longer there.

"I wasn't trying to ... I mean ... I wasn't insinuating ... can't you stay?"

"I really have to go," she called from inside the house.

Mr. Boogie barked, and Efram walked around the wrap-around porch to watch her leave. "Bye," he said lightly, as Joy ran down the steps. She answered back and waved. Her hair swayed in the wind, back and forth like a tick-tock clock. Efram watched as her thin figure disappeared into the woods.

The wind chimes dinged a little song as Efram yanked a flower from a vine and slowly pulled off the petals until it was bare. He walked over to the open window and leaned into it while the curtains lapped at his face. Inside, the large canvas stood almost erect against the piano. Efram held the little flower bud in front of his eye, squinting like a photographer ready to shoot. He smiled.

Chapter 8

Summer Savory

"**E**veryone read the chapter? Those who did look up from your book," Joy's teacher asked the class. Joy watched her teacher circle the podium like a politician about to make an all-too-important point. "You're all liars," the teacher said as all the students looked up. The class laughed, but Joy felt left out of the joke. Her mind was on Efram and her Friday visit. Had he been about to kiss her? Why had she ran? Even throughout dinner with her family that night, she had stared at the walls, lifting the fork to her mouth more like a machine than a hungry person.

"Oh, just thinking," she had answered when her mother inquired about her stupefied look.

"Homework, dear?" Beverly had asked.

"Yeah ... yeah ... um ... lots ... I should get to work." Joy had left the table and spent the rest of the evening on her bed daydreaming. For some reason, she thought of Efram dancing. Then she thought about him painting, sitting so peacefully in front of his canvas near the lake. She wanted to come up behind him and put her hands on his shoulders, knead them. She was thinking, as well, that her family would not approve.

The thud of book bags hitting desktops jarred Joy back to the present. The students were leaving. She leaned over to the student beside her to ask about homework. None. Joy smiled and headed for the door.

Outside, Efram's car whirred into the parking lot. Finding a spot, he looked around and watched the students come and go. It brought back bad memories of teachers he thought were ignorant and students who were hopeless. He climbed out and propped himself up on the hood, letting one leg dangle off the side. With his black jeans, red T-shirt, black boots, and RayBans, he looked like a *Rolling Stone* cover boy.

Patiently he waited, and soon enough Joy appeared. Her hair was pulled back in a pink ribbon. Efram enjoyed the tight jeans that hugged her body and the white V-neck T-shirt that outlined her breasts. Her sandals clicked on the pavement as she hurried for the sidewalk, not seeing Efram. He whistled. Joy turned around and her mouth fell open. He grinned, motioning her over with his hand. With her thumb, she pointed to herself. Efram stood up and imitated a cop directing traffic. Shaking her head and smiling, Joy walked toward him. As she got closer, she noticed the sweat beading up on his arm and imagined that his jeans must be stuck to his legs after sitting in the hot sun.

"I've come to bring *you* a peace offering," Efram said and held open the door. "I've got a picnic basket, Evian, white grape juice, and even a blanket. Left Mr. Boogie at home."

"How the hell ... how did you ... how long have you been here?" Joy let her book bag fall to the ground.

"Oh, I haven't been here long. Ready?"

"How'd you know when to pick me up?"

"Well, it's lunch time! And, I'm taking you to lunch." Efram took her bag and opened the door for her. "Madam."

"Ouch!" she yelled when her body touched the sun-warmed seat.

"It's a bit hot." He threw her bag into the back and hopped into the car. "Actually, this is a bit earlier than when you visited me Friday, so I assumed you'd be out soon. Remarkably, I have the ability to reason."

"Splendid, Mr. Holmes," she said, admiring his cleverness.

Efram smiled. "Tunes?"

"What d'ya have?" She rummaged through his CD holder. Motown, Duke Ellington, Elton John, Chopin, Tina Turner. "Abba?" Joy held up one of the discs.

Efram took it from her and flipped it over his shoulder and into the back seat. "Uh, yeah, how 'bout something else?"

Choosing a Jackie Wilson greatest-hits compilation, Joy inserted the CD. The sun reflected on the disc, and Efram squinted when a ray rebounded into his eye. The LED lit up as Joy flipped to *Higher and Higher*.

"That's my favorite," she said and bopped her head to the beat. "Hey, I thought Boogie traveled everywhere with you."

Efram chuckled and revved up the car so quickly that Joy fell back in her seat. "Not everywhere," he said. He drove to the freeway on-ramp and pulled onto the interstate. He leaned back, throwing his hand casually over the steering wheel, while his right hand relaxed on the gear shift in much the same way as it had the evening he rescued her from the rain. Joy clasped her hands in her lap and watched his fingers tap the gear shift. It was like he was tapping out a Morse code, going along with the beat of the music. The song flowed out of the speakers, into their ears, and into their private thoughts.

Efram was excited – like the first time you go on a school field trip, you know it's going to be fun, but you have no idea what to expect. Joy, on the other hand, felt like a heroine from a romance novel, being whisked away by a handsome stranger. Here she was, Joy Baxter, out with a man she'd had a handful of previous encounters with, only one being meaningful.

As the song played and the wind caressed her face, Joy smiled, while Efram kept his eyes glued to the road, lost in thought himself. Joy watched his lips whisper the words to the song, wondering what his mouth felt like, thinking about his painting of the lake – the rhythm of it, the movement, the tenderness.

The song neared its end, and she reached over to switch to another, accidentally touching Efram's hand. For her, it could just as easily have been an electric eel. Efram turned and smiled. With his dark glasses, he looked like a movie star. Joy blushed and changed the song to *Baby Workout*.

The sweat started to show on her chest, making her shirt stick to her body. She squirmed to loosen the material, then pulled her hair into a tighter ponytail. Even with the car top down, nothing could contain the heat. She leaned her head over the side and let the air hit her in the face. The wind cooled her neck.

Efram watched her and clutched the gear shift. His hand, wet with sweat, easily slid back and forth over the gear shift. His lips were covered in droplets of sweat as well, and he tasted the sweet salt that gathered there, imagining it was the liquid dripping down Joy's neck and between her breasts. A lump gathered in his throat; his pants felt tighter. He tugged, mostly pinched, at the jeans that were stuck to his body.

Joy twisted a strand of hair that had fallen out of her ponytail, pretending not to notice Efram's gaze. The chemistry in the air was so strong not even Mount Olympus could have contained its elements. The energy hovered like a heavy weight.

Caught in her magnetism and lost in thought, it took a car honking in the next lane to jerk Efram back to reality. "It's not much farther now," he said and pulled off the interstate.

They drove about a mile before venturing down a long, curvy road covered with potholes and gravel. The car bumped along and Efram removed the CD that was skipping from the harsh ride.

"And exactly how did you find this place?" Joy asked.

Efram laughed. "Okay, it's where I once buried a man." He looked at her, waiting for a reaction, but Joy just rolled her eyes. "All right, I've never actually been here, but my agent told me about it. Said it would be a good place for inspiration, neglecting to tell me it's bad for my car. He does that a lot."

The air began to smell like water; they could see a reflection through the tree limbs. When they reached the lake, Efram parked the car as near to the pier as he could and looked at Joy. "Buried him right over there." Joy smirked and climbed out of the car. Efram reached for the picnic basket. "Hey, I hope you like what I brought. It's a veggie sandwich – Swiss, avocado, tomato, lettuce, bell pepper, sprouts, and hot mustard for added tang."

"Sounds fine," she said and added, "Are you a health nut?"

"Not strictly, but I try to eat healthy. Sometimes I splurge though."

"Too bad we didn't bring a canoe. Or a swim suit. That water looks so inviting."

Efram slung the blanket over his shoulder and grimaced. "Swim in that thing? Snakes and all?"

"Ya ain't much of a country boy, 'er ya?"

He nodded his head and said, "I told ya I was born and raised." He handed Joy the Evian and the grape juice as she walked around to his side of the car. "But I prefer them cement ponds," Efram added with a Southern drawl.

"When did you move to New York?" she asked as they walked towards the pier. The marshy soil immediately stuck to their shoes. Joy's toes slid around in her sandals as the ground became even mushier when they approached the pier.

Efram looked up at the sky. "Moved to New York when I was eighteen to go to college. Dropped out, though. Boring."

Joy jumped onto the warped wood and looked at the water bobbing beneath her like a small wave in the ocean, though it smelled more like mildew mixed with pine and wildflowers. Her nose twitched. "So what'd you do after that?"

"Hung out. Played in a band. Worked on my art." Efram spread out the wool army blanket and smoothed it with his hand. He got down on his knees and began unloading the basket. Each item was in Tupperware or wrapped in aluminum foil. Joy plopped down across from him and peered into the basket. Efram playfully slapped her hand and shook his finger, then placed a paper plate and a red plastic cup in front of her.

"Juice or water?" he asked.

"Water." She wrinkled her forehead, confused, while Efram poured. "No wine?"

"I don't drink."

"You a teetotaler?"

"No, an alcoholic." He put ice in the drinks as nonchalantly as he said it.

"Oh." She rubbed her neck.

Taking out two carefully wrapped sandwiches, he placed them on their plates. As he popped open each Tupperware container, he took a deep breath, smelling the contents like a connoisseur testing wine. "Let the picnicking begin, Boo Boo," he said and rubbed his palms together.

Joy took a bite of the sandwich. With her mouth full, she said, "Do you still have family in Arkansas?"

"Some aunts and uncles. My parents have been dead for three years."

"I'm sorry. My Dad died several years ago of a heart attack."

Efram gave her a mournful grin. "Hurts."

"Yeah."

"I was in New York at the time. Smoke alarm didn't go off. I'm sure Dad never changed the batteries. Probably didn't know it needed a battery. Idiot."

Unsure what to say, she quickly changed the subject, "I don't know why anyone would choose to live here over New York."

"New York is fun, but everyone in my world was obsessed with being on the society page. Obsessed about wearing the right clothes. Stupid. They say they like my stuff, but they like the idea of my stuff. They like it in their living room. Status symbol. Why not just take a picture of their bank statement? It got to the point, Joy, that I could take a crayon and draw an X on construction paper and it would sell because it had my name on it. That's crazy."

"So you think people here aren't superficial? It ain't better. Everyone here just ... well ... exists. Why would you want to *walk* through life when you could be *jumping around* in it?"

"I know. Live. Die. Add up your money at the end. Life isn't Monopoly."

"Yeah. Sucks." Joy pulled the crusts from her sandwich and threw them into the lake.

"So, how do you survive?" he asked.

Joy pondered for a moment until a bluebird, slowly edging toward them hoping for a crumb, broke her concentration. Efram tossed it a piece of bread; the bird jumped back a few steps.

"Here, birdie, birdie, we won't bite," Efram said, slowly getting up to walk closer. The bird cocked its head, wondering if the tall human was serious. Efram squatted; Joy came up behind him and placed her hands on his shoulders, making him grin. He was glad she was behind him. The bird fluttered its wings but didn't move away, so Efram scooted the bread a little closer and waited. It chirped and bounced even closer. Giving Efram and Joy one final look, it clutched the bread in its beak and flew off. They watched until it was out of view.

Joy returned to the picnic blanket, poured a glass of Evian, and dropped in three cubes from the small bag of ice. "Really hot," she said.

Efram put his hands in his pockets and watched her.

"What?" she asked, noticing that his gaze had shifted to something behind her.

He walked over to the wooden post that supported the dock. "Stand on this," he said and patted the top of it which came to Efram's waist. "It'll make a great shot. Let me get my camera." He started for the car, but Joy grabbed the tail of his shirt.

"Are you nuts, Efram? I can't balance on that!"

Efram pulled away and kept going. Joy sat back down and watched his legs sprint to the car, the jeans flexing with him. He leaned over the door, and she continued to admire him. A 35-millimeter camera over his shoulder, he ran back and grabbed Joy's shoulder.

"Come on. Up," he said. Joy grunted and crossed her arms. Efram smirked. "Please. I'll make you a star." He gave her that mischievous smile she couldn't resist.

"Yeah, I bet you say that to all the girls."

"Only the pretty ones."

Blushing, Joy stood up. "You want me to stand on this?" The diameter of the post was no bigger than the balls of her feet.

Efram put the camera down on the blanket, then put his hands on her waist to help her up. She liked the way his hands felt on her body. Face to face, they stood for a moment before he lifted her. She could feel the top of the post and tapped it with the tip of her sandals.

"No sandals. Too slippery," she said and fell back into Efram's grasp.

She took off the mud-caked sandals and dusted off the bottoms of her feet. She arched her back to stretch before Efram hoisted her again. When she leaned forward, he held on to her outstretched hands, helping her to balance. She stood there with her butt in the air and one foot over the other. They both grinned, about to giggle. It looked like something Norman Rockwell would have painted if he'd lived in the 1990s: two people, dressed casually in T-shirts and jeans, enjoying a picnic, having some fun, and falling in love.

Slowly, Efram let go of Joy's hands. He held her hips until she was able to steady herself by holding her arms out like an acrobat on a high beam. Like a movie director scoping out a shot, he formed two letter L's with his hands. Then he crept backwards and picked up his camera, never taking his eyes off her.

"Now, could you pose for me?" he asked.

Joy's eyes widened. "Pardon? Pose? How? I'm up here, aren't I? End of the deal."

"Yeah, but you look kinda silly ... um ... put your hands behind your neck or stretch them above your head." Efram focused the lens.

"I don't think so. *You* wanna do this?"

Efram looked at her through the lens. Joy tried to position herself in the way he wanted. Click. Click. "That looks great. Now ... "

Joy hovered on the post for a second, screamed, and toppled backwards into the lake. Dropping his camera, Efram dived in and wrapped one arm around her, pulling her back up. She swung her hair around; the water hit him in the face. She gasped for air and rested her head on his shoulder as he lifted her to the dock. Safely on the pier, Joy twined her legs around his waist as Efram bobbed up and down in the water.

Her bra showed through the wet T-shirt, and Efram tried not to look. "You all right?" he asked. She started to giggle and cough. Efram twirled his tongue in his mouth, raised his eyebrows, and pulled himself out of the water. "I risk life and limb for you and you laugh."

"Yeah, the snakes could've gotten you." She punched his arm. Efram toppled over, then popped back up like a Fisher-Price Weeble toy. He reached into the water and pulled out his floating sunglasses. He found a napkin and wiped them.

As she started to use her shirt to wipe the water from her face, she noticed the see-through effect. Pretending not to be aware, she pulled out the tail of her shirt and wiped her face anyway, exposing part of her stomach. A tiny pouch of flesh sat on the edge of her jeans. Her belly button, filled with water, sat on top as if peeking out for air. Catching Efram's gaze, Joy pulled her shirt down, folded her arms over her chest, and straightened her back.

Efram looked around. "I've got a towel, I think," he said and walked to the car. When he returned, he threw the towel at her, letting it smack her in the face. It only made her laugh at him again.

"Are you angry? You know it was *your* idea to do that!" she said.

"Well, at least we got cooled off. The sun should have us dry in a few minutes."

A few bees hovered by the food, and Efram shooed them away. Joy watched him swat at the insects with his bare hands. She ducked and hid under the towel when they came for her. The bees swirled around the picnic until they got tired of Efram's pestering. Smiling, he straightened the blanket and motioned for Joy to join him for the rest of the lunch. As she moved toward him, a bee landed on her arm and stung her. Joy screamed and smashed the insect. Its stinger remained in her arm; the pain seared into her skin like barbed wire. Grabbing a tissue, Efram removed the stinger.

"I saw some summer savory over by the car. It'll help," he told her.

Joy wrinkled her forehead and looked at her swelling arm. Efram returned, crushing some leaves in his palm. He smoothed them on her skin.

"Thank you," she said, smiling.

Sensing her next question, he replied, "I was once a witch doctor."

"Witch doctors in Arkansas?"

"Yeah, loads."

After her arm felt better, he handed her a chocolate brownie, and Joy asked, "How come you aren't scared of bees? You're scared of those other bugs."

"So?" Efram licked chocolate from his fingers.

"So? How come?"

"I'm not scared of anything."

"Except those bugs."

Efram looked her in the eye. "Don't count."

"Why? That's crazy." Legs pulled up against her, Joy rocked on her bottom while she bit into the brownie.

"There's only one thing that really scares me," he said.

"And that is?"

"Losing control."

"Efram Corbet, always in control."

"Not always." He got up and stretched his legs, staring at the tree tops. A bird flew low; then Efram watched it soar. It stopped at the very top of a tree, and he could barely see a nest. Faintly, he heard birds chirping.

Joy reached into the basket for another brownie. "You didn't really answer my question."

He smiled and sat back down. "I just don't like bugs."

She laughed. "Or losing control."

"Yeah." He stared at her for a long while, enjoying the amused look on her face. Her hair was turning kinky as it dried. He so wanted to smooth it back, feel the silky strands, or take a piece into his mouth and suck off the remaining wetness. In his life, he had met a lot of typical beauties, but of all the people, Joy was very different. Like Mona Lisa, something was underneath her exterior, beyond her smile, that screamed masterpiece.

"Joy, I have be honest. I have an ulterior motive for bringing you here."

"What?" Joy asked, her mouth full. Crumbs dropped from her fingers and she flicked them away as they fell onto her pants. "I'm not getting up on another one of those posts."

"No." Efram laughed. "To sweeten you up before ... " He took the brownie from her hand.

"Hey, wait a minute ... sweeten me up for what?"

Efram took a deep breath, hoping she didn't notice his reserve. "I ... well, would like to paint you." Efram smiled, a small grin really, like a child hoping no one would notice the stolen cookie crumbs around his mouth.

"Paint me?" Joy put her hand to her chest and noticed that her bra still showed through the fabric. Nonchalantly, she lifted the shirt from her skin and pretended to fan herself.

"Sure, why not? You're a good subject. A local yokel." Efram let out his cocky laugh, while his thoughts focused on Joy and Joy only, not about her place in a small town.

"What kind of painting?" Joy pulled at the bottom of her T-shirt.

She wanted to pose for Efram Corbet more than she had wanted anything in a long time.

"Just a portrait. That's all."

"Oh. Well, what kind of portrait?"

"Kind?"

"I mean ... you know ... "

Efram let his head fall back as he laughed. He pointed at her, but Joy wasn't laughing. "Nude, eh? Is that what you thought?" Efram envisioned her in front of his canvas. He knew she would merge perfectly, seamlessly, with soft colors and the bare canvas. He turned to stare at the picnic basket, chuckling off the last of his laughter.

"Well, I didn't ... you know ... art class ... "

"Oh, yeah, college-art girl. No, you know, just a portrait." The sun hitting him in the eye, he still caught her blush. "I pay really well. College students always need cash. So, what's it gonna be?"

"When?"

Efram started packing the basket, neatly folding the dirty napkins. "How 'bout this weekend, if you like?"

"I ... I ... guess ... "

"Great." After packing away most of the stuff from the picnic, he looked at her, his eyes following the inseam of her jeans as it bunched up at her crotch. She was still sitting with her legs close to her body. Efram raised his eyebrows. "I'll pick you up at noon then? Saturday."

Joy shrugged her shoulders. "I can just walk to your house. No big deal."

"I can swing by, Joy."

"No, really, I'll walk. Gotta walk off these brownies." She patted her belly, rubbed it, then thumped it like a melon.

"Sure." Efram shrugged and got up. She certainly had no fat to work off. Gathering up the picnic basket and tugging on the blanket Joy was still sitting on, he nodded. Joy hopped up and straightened her still-damp clothes, trying to think of an excuse in case anyone was home when he dropped her off. Efram flung the blanket over his shoulder and walked towards the car.

"You can pick me up if you want, but it's a nice walk through the woods and I like it." Joy ran up behind him and rubbed his back. Quickly she stopped herself, clenching her hand like someone hiding an M&M.

"You're ashamed to be seen with me," he said as he got to the car. "Go on. Admit it." Throwing the stuff in the back seat, he turned to face her.

Joy's eyes widened. "No way."

"Yep. That's it." Without opening the door, he jumped into the car. "Imagine that. A girl ashamed to be with me."

"Yeah, imagine that." The horn bellowed as Joy walked in front of the car. Efram laughed and Joy slapped the hood.

"Hey, watch it, girlie. You wanna polish that?"

Joy opened the door and sat down. "You got paw prints on your hood."

"Active dog."

"Very."

The car started; Efram backed out, careful not to hit any bumps. Shaking her head, Joy thought about being alone with him again.

Chapter 9

Passion Flower

"Efram, you got the noodles?" Joy stood over the boiling pot as Efram tossed the salad into the air. The music was so loud she screamed it again. "Noodles, Efram! Where are the noodles?"

Efram pranced over to the cabinet like a Mexican hat-dancer. "Zi newdells zey hera." He opened the cabinet and danced away, juggling the salad without spilling a leaf.

"Que?"

Efram turned down the portable CD player. "No more somba?"

"Si." Joy unwrapped the plastic covering and dropped the pasta into the steaming water. The noodles sizzled, flinging tiny balls of water onto the stove.

"You no like somba?" he asked. "You just jealous 'cause I dance better than you, senorita." Shaking the oil and vinegar bottle, he hummed the rest of the song. "I show you how." He scooted closer to Joy. She shook her head and held up her hands. "Oh, don't be shy, Joy." Efram turned the CD back up. He wiggled his hips and put down the bottle. His head bopped in time with the song.

"Efram, you call that dancing?"

"Oh, better, are we?" He snapped his fingers in the air.

"With better music. I thought you had better taste," Joy yelled over the sound of the music and the raging water.

"I like all music." He stopped and scratched his head. "Except country. Just don't get it. Too many trailer parks and beer bottles for me."

Joy turned the stove down, letting the boiling water simmer, and walked up to Efram. "You wanna dance?" she asked, snapping her fingers.

"Si!" He started to put his arm around her, but Joy held up her hand. She pushed the stop button on the CD player and went into the living room. Squatting on the floor, she rummaged through his compact discs until she found Sam Cooke.

"You like to cha-cha, eh?" she asked.

Efram raised his eyebrows, leaning against the piano, grinning. After sliding in the disc, the song started and Joy jumped up. She flicked her head to the side and motioned for Efram to dance with her. Looking around, he wrinkled his forehead and pointed to himself. Putting her hands in front of her, she motioned for him as if she were pulling a tug-of-war rope. She danced and spun around, pretending that she was wearing a hoop skirt. She flicked her wrists as she circled him. Efram slipped his hand around her waist and pulled her against him. As the music danced with the sunset becoming visible in the darkening room, Joy and Efram twirled around, almost stepping on Mr. Boogie. The little dog grunted and left the room.

"Flat footing!" Efram cried. Joy raised her eyebrows and took off her shoes. They jumped up and down like on a trampoline, then continued their dance. Joy walked around him and clapped her hands to the beat of the song. Grabbing her by the arm, he pulled her close, then released her, letting her twirl away. With his arm stretched as far as it would go, he tugged her back, trying to be graceful.

"Not bad, Ef," she said in mid-spin. The "Ef" rolled out of her mouth so easily. In her daydreams, she called him that. Efram continued to dance, seeming to ignore the nickname.

She hoped her mother didn't discover that she had lied about finding a job. All she needed was for her mother to walk into the children's department at Sears, hoping for a lunch date with her daughter, and not find her. Joy hadn't even told her family until Thursday night, when she blurted out, between bites of a ham sandwich, that she had to train for her new job over the weekend. Her mother's eyes widened. Fortunately, her sisters ignored her, Katie thumbing through *Teen Beat* while Emily watched television.

The rest of the week, while she pondered what to tell the family, she had fantasized about the painting. She visualized it hanging in a gallery, being admired by socialites, while she and Efram stood beside it arm in arm. Sometimes she thought of the future, like something from *Star Trek*, with people dressed in silver pulling up her painting on a computer screen and analyzing it for a college art-history class. For the most part, her daydreams turned romantic. She imagined Efram kissing her, strolling with her through Paris, and showing her the world. Then she thought about him coming up behind her, picnic basket in hand, while she sat in front of the Sphinx, plugging information into her notebook computer.

She had not been without reservations, however. The thought of having Efram, basically a total stranger, stare at her for hours and days was a bit unnerving. For all she knew, he was a pervert, but her instincts told her better, and as she twirled in Efram's arms she was positive he was perfect.

He smiled as the song came to an end. "What's next?" Joy asked. The compact disc player answered for her by moving quickly to the next tune. "Hey, Ef, can you twist?" Joy twisted her bare feet on the floor, making squeaking sounds. Efram followed her lead and they did the twist together, getting sweaty and laughing.

The moon was out but the day was still fighting. And they were fighting, too – fighting the work that still hadn't been done on their first day of painting. By the time the fourth track came on, they were already shamelessly exhausted. Efram stopped dancing and fell down to the floor, spread-eagled. "I'm pooped. Maybe next one's a slow jam," he said, raising his head. He crawled over to the stereo while Joy leaned on the back of the couch. He smiled. "Let's just skip to the next one," he said. Joy walked to the center of the living room like she knew what song was next. She stood there, bare feet, cut-off shorts, and midriff shirt. He ran to her and put his arms around her again. She looked up at him. He blew a piece of hair out of his face. With her palms she rubbed his shoulders, as the song began with a declaration of love. Joy looked down. Efram looked past her at the blank canvas. He could feel her breath against his chest.

As she gazed at his chest through two open buttons, Joy wanted to kiss his bare skin. As the song progressed, she felt herself moving closer to him. Through his black jeans, she could feel him. She shivered.

"You okay, Joy?" he asked and looked down at the top of her head. Her hair was shiny like bronze. Little beads of sweat had dripped onto her shoulders. He wanted to lick it off, let the tip of his tongue drop into it like a tiny needle poking an atom – just enough to sample, but not enough to disturb.

"Um, Efram, I think the noodles are burning." She pulled partly away, her hands still resting on his chest.

"Yeah, I'd hate for the noodles to overcook. Why don't you go check? I'll get the CD."

Joy stepped back, letting her hand slip down his stomach, not realizing what she was doing. Stopping at his belt loops, she walked away. Efram watched her until she was gone. He bowed his head and went to the stereo to turn off the music. He lingered for a moment, letting the song come to an end on its own.

The first day of painting and nothing had been accomplished, except a boiling pot of pasta. Efram was satisfied, however. He had been sketching Joy from memory all week, trying to decide on a pose. By late Thursday night, as he watched an A&E special on Greek mythology, he had an idea. The rest of the night, he mixed colors and visualized exactly where Joy would sit. On Friday, he quickly sewed Joy an outfit, a sheer white gown with buttonholes through which he looped a long string of the material. It looked like a mixture of a soft silk bodice and a negligee – very "Parrishesque," he thought. He feared she would think it too sheer, so all day he put off the work, instead showing her some of his favorite paintings in an art book. Before he realized it, the day was over, but he didn't want Joy to leave. Knowing there was plenty of pasta in the kitchen, he invited her to stay for dinner.

Going back into the kitchen, Efram saw Joy pouring the steaming noodles into a colander in the sink. "Ze newdells zey red-dee," she said and smiled.

"Great. I'll set the table." He began removing dishes from the cabinet, as she hummed the remainder of the Sam Cooke tune. "You're not such a bad little dancer, Joy, but your Spanish needs work."

Joy shook the noodles to drain off the water. "And that was Spanish, or was it French, you were attempting earlier?"

"Spanish!"

"Very good. Very, very good." After putting tongs in the noodles, she placed the bowl on the table, careful not to cover the tablecloth's embroidered red passion flower.

"Okay, I'm not bilingual."

"No? I wouldn't have ... "

"Okay. No need for sarcasm," he said as he placed the dishes on the table. "Actually, the only French I know is deja vu."

"Dingy people get that a lot."

Efram, who had started looking in the bottom cabinets, shut one of the doors, and edged closer to Joy. "You're something of a little smart ass, aren't you?"

"I have my moments." Joy poured the sauce into a white china bowl and continued, "I know some foreign words. Bonjour and merci. There are a lot of familiar words. What else is pretty common?" Efram shrugged and continued to search the cabinets before moving to the drawers. Joy watched him. "Efram, what the hell are you looking for?" He mumbled and she asked him again.

"Candles," he said and walked into the living room.

Joy smiled, knowing he couldn't see her. How romantic, she thought. She could hear him rattling more drawers. As she finished arranging the food and the dishes, he returned holding two long, white candles and two gold candle holders. He held them up like a Viking returning from a successful pillage. Joy held out her hand, motioning for him to have a seat. He obliged after lighting the candles at the stove burner. The two sat down and Efram took a deep breath. He put his elbows on the table as if he was about to pray.

"Je t'aime," he said.

Joy stumbled on her words. "Par ... don?"

"Yeah, that, too." He unfolded his napkin and placed it in his lap. "A familiar French word."

"Oh, yeah, I forgot that one," she lied.

Chapter 10

Black-Eyed Susan

"**You** like this job, Joy?" her mother asked. "You stayed so late. Aren't you tired? You shouldn't let it affect your studies, dear."

Joy smiled and went to her room, carrying the Sunday paper under her arm. Her bed was covered with books, heavy like an iron blanket. She dreaded climbing in and starting on her homework. Her desk was littered with balled-up paper from a report she just couldn't seem to get through. In the center of the desk, an ink spot remained from a leaky pen. She had chewed the end off the night before, wondering why Efram hadn't begun the painting on Saturday, or at least told her what it was going to be like.

Frowning, she got into bed, dislodging the books. She grunted at the loud sound as the books smacked the floor. The fan, always turned on, cooled her face as she stared at the book covers. Reluctantly, she leaned over, grabbed the geology text and opened it. Her paper was due in a week, but working with Efram would cut into her time. She could not justify putting it off any longer.

"Yo, girl, how's your job?" Katie asked, dragging her feet as she entered the room. She dropped onto Joy's bed, landing like an anchor as the book bobbed up and down like a fishing cork.

"Once again, you fail to understand the meaning of privacy." Joy rolled over and raised herself on her elbows.

"It was open." Katie picked up Joy's textbook and began fanning the pages. "So, guess what?" she asked. Joy shook her head. Katie laughed under her breath, nervous like a new mobster after a kill, then scooted closer to Joy. "I have a secret, but ... "

"You have a secret butt? I don't think so. That ass is huge. They can see it on Mars."

"Must you always be a smart ass?"

"Funny. Someone else told me that recently, so I guess I am."

Katie sighed. "Please, this is serious."

"All right. What's the secret? What's this about?"

Katie got up and paced. Joy sat up. "What is it?"

Katie laughed, gasping for air, while Joy stared at her. "Crazy, really. You were right. I have been behaving badly, and it's come back to haunt me." She threw her arms in the air, closed the door, and turned to look at Joy. Katie's lip was quivering like a child's scared of the Boogie Man.

Joy got off the bed. "What are you talking about?"

"I gotta tell somebody, but you can't tell Mom or Emily. Emily would just lecture and Mom would have a cow."

Joy rubbed her sister's back, something she hadn't done since they were both kids, when Katie proclaimed Joy the world's champion massager.

"Are you ready for this?" Katie walked over to the desk and started cleaning up the wadded paper. "I'm pregnant."

Joy stood there as if she'd just been told she was dead, knowing it was impossible. "Katie, are you sure?" Joy stumbled through the questions in her head unsure what to ask or say next.

"I'm sure." Katie fiddled with the pens in Joy's Chicago Bulls cup. "I took a pregnancy test. You know, from the drugstore." With her thumb, she pointed towards town. "Positive. I waited a week and broke down and went to see Dr. Carter. You know, the cute one who is friends with Mom's podiatrist."

"So it's positive. How far along?"

Katie smirked. "Three months now." Twisting the cover of Joy's notebook, she looked back at her sister, who was leaning against the bedpost with her mouth open.

"Who's the dad?" Joy asked. Katie was silent. "Don't tell me you don't know!"

"Shit, Joy, of course."

Joy stared at her, knowing Katie was lying, because every time she lied her eyebrow twitched.

"Joy, does it really matter?"

Joy threw back her head. "Ugh, Katie! Are you going to tell Mom?" Katie started pacing again. "You have to! This is not the kind of secret you can keep. Mom's going to get suspicious when she sees that rotund belly start protruding."

"Just give me time to think."

"What are you going to do? Abortion? Isn't it too late?"

"No! I'm keeping it!"

"Katie, you're still in school – too young to have a baby."

"You never do anything wrong, do you, Miss Perfect?" The balled-up paper on Joy's desk slid into the chair as Katie shoved them.

"This ain't about me."

"Just don't tell anyone! Can you at least promise me that?"

Joy sucked in her cheeks, trying to contain her words like a spy on the hot seat. "Whatever."

"Thank you. Give me time to think of a way to tell Mom."

Joy shook her head and began to pick up the paper from her desk chair. Katie stood by the desk, toying with a doily that had belonged to their grandmother. "Remember when I used to use this for Barbie's dollhouse rug?" Katie asked.

"Yeah." Joy continued to clean her desk. They heard a pan fall to the floor in the kitchen.

"Sometimes Mom's so clumsy when she washes dishes. I'm surprised we have glasses to drink from. Better go help." As Katie left, Joy sighed and rolled pencils under her palm. Her books beckoned her, but her mind was not focused on finding ancient dinosaur bones or ancient civilizations. The hell from Revelations could not compete with the eruption soon to hit her home. It wasn't her problem, she reasoned, and walked over to her bed and picked up her books. Her life was fine. She was going to a good university and wouldn't have to worry about it. And, she had a Efram. This was Katie's mess. It was destined to happen to

Katie anyway. She had always been on that path. Everything in life happens for a reason, Joy thought, and everything is as it should be. Maybe, Joy thought for a moment, this would ultimately be the best thing that ever happened to Katie. Maybe.

Rummaging through her desk drawer, she found a purse-size bottle of Tylenol. She pulled a water bottle out of her book bag and took two tablets. The water was warm, and Joy gagged as the pills went down with it. Reluctantly, she organized her thoughts to start work on her paper.

Eventually she fell asleep at the desk, only to be startled awake by Katie's stereo. Her mother hollered at Katie to turn it down. Joy rolled her head and rubbed her neck. It was nearly dark. She popped her knuckles and stared out her window, which faced the woods. She smiled as she remembered her dream – she and Efram were at the lake dancing to *You've Really Got a Hold on Me*. In her dream, Efram's long fingers, as thin as the reeds swaying in the marsh, caressed her back. She had started to close her eyes again when suddenly she saw headlights through the pine trees – trees so thick the lights looked like tiny hovering flashlights. It looked as if they were headed towards Efram's house, and she wondered if it was his car. Getting up from her desk, Joy tried to open the window, forgetting that it had been stuck since she was five years old. Joy had been examining arrowheads, or what she thought were arrowheads, that she had dug up near the driveway, when she heard giggling outside. She had looked out and saw Emily kissing a red-haired boy that Joy knew from the drugstore. Joy had been watching for only a few seconds before Emily caught her snooping and ran into the house. Before she knew it, Emily was in her room and slammed down the window. Joy hadn't been able to open it since.

The lights disappeared as her mother knocked on the door.

"Joy, dinner."

"Coming." Taking one last look out the window, catching a black-eyed susan moving seductively in the breeze, Joy sighed, wishing she was with Efram.

Chapter 11

Heartsease

Usually, waiting for Joy made Efram feel like a butterfly testing its wings for the first time. She made him excited, ready to experience flight. Now, he was tense. Joy wasn't expected for another hour, which gave him plenty of time to tidy up the house after last night's rage, but he couldn't concentrate. He didn't know what to tell Joy, or even if he should. Really, it wasn't her business. After nearly dropping a paint can on Mr. Boogie, he stopped cleaning and sat down on the piano stool. A lemon icebox pie was chilling in the refrigerator, a dessert for Joy that he had picked up last night after Alana left. He contemplated eating it without her as he touched the keys on the piano, gently enough not to make any noise. As he sat there, his mind kept replaying last night's events like a hot-wired VCR. Throughout his life he had run away from bad memory after bad memory, allowing the thoughts to bulge up until he created art – that was when it was safe, because he had control; he could start and stop at anytime. Now, as he sat there, he thought of Alana, who was still as haggard as when he had last seen her at a friend's art show in January. The thought of her was stagnant in his mind like a piece of slime clinging to the edges of a stopped-up toilet bowl. Suddenly, for no reason, he shivered. "An angel must have flown by," he said, pressing his fingers onto the keys so that they rang as if in the halls of a church. "Joy will be here soon. Gotta clean up."

Efram resumed cleaning and picked up the empty paint cans, which he had thrown across the room after Alana left, and took them to the back porch. Returning to the living room, he carefully removed pieces of glass – all that was left of a vase, a gift Alana had brought back from her recent trip to Mexico. He dropped the pieces into the trash. The glass broke again as it hit the bottom of the pail; Efram shuddered when he heard it.

To change the mood of the house, he turned on the same Sam Cooke CD he and Joy had danced to on Saturday. *You Send Me* pervaded the room like a pleasing perfume. He sat down at the piano and played along with the tune.

When Joy arrived, she saw Efram's head bowed and his back to her. She noticed a few pieces of glass on the floor and saw that a painting was slightly tilted. She was curious. Undetected, Joy approached Efram. The pounding of the keys deafened him to her footsteps. She wrapped her hands over his eyes and was startled to feel his tears. Efram gasped and jumped to his feet, knocking over the piano stool. He never said a word. He merely put his arms around her waist and gently kissed her.

After the kiss, he stared at her. The tears had reddened his eyes. He started to turn away, then yanked her closer, clutching her back tightly. Again he kissed her, this time slipping his tongue into her mouth. Joy's feet nearly left the floor. Roughly, he ran his hands up and down her back. Her fingers shook as she kneaded his shoulders, feeling the cool cotton of his shirt.

When he released her, Joy took a deep breath. Efram stepped over the stool before he bent down to pick it up. Joy stared at him and continued to relive the moment by running her tongue against the roof of her mouth, never wanting to forget the feeling.

"I'm sorry," Efram muttered. "I get carried away." He ran his hands through his hair and looked around the room at nothing.

Joy couldn't respond. Caught up in the kiss, she had temporarily forgotten about his tear-stained eyes. She wanted to know why he was crying, but did not want to pry.

Efram wiped his face. "Are we going to create some art or what?" He pointed to the kitchen. "I've got lemon pie for dessert. Since you're early, let's get started, then tackle lunch."

Joy went to the bathroom to change, still in shock from what had happened.

Efram knocked on the door. Very quietly he said, "Joy, please don't be mad, but this painting is supposed to be romantic. You can't wear anything underneath the outfit. It's really not as sheer as it looks."

Joy's eyes widened. The material *was* very sheer. She held the thin fabric in her hand and rubbed it between her fingers. Still tingling from the kiss, she did not care if her breasts peeked through the material.

Efram arranged his supplies, trying to erase any evidence from last night's ordeal. When she returned wearing the sheer white outfit, he tried not to stare at her, but she looked beautiful. He pointed to the window seat, which had a great view of the lake. When she sat on the window seat, and he behind the easel, Joy felt completely naked. She tried covering her chest in an obvious way with her arms, but her breasts peeked through the thin fabric and there was no way to conceal them. He got up from his little paint-covered stool to position her just the right way. She leaned back, a little scared, and he placed her right arm over her head. Her left hand he let dangle, holding a red rose. The floor at her feet was now covered in white roses. Efram explained that he would add a red rose to them each day.

"Won't that affect the outcome? How will it look finished? All white or all red flowers?" Joy asked.

"That all depends on you." He returned to his easel. "Don't pose. No smile, frown, or anything. Just look."

The position, while it looked natural, was uncomfortable. Joy didn't think she could hold it. She was embarrassed and her eyes watered from staring at him. After only a few minutes, she stretched, and Efram yelled, "Stay!"

Joy laughed. "What am I? A dog?"

Efram shook his head. "Just be still, girl."

Joy wanted to twist her head and look out the window, but instead was forced to stare at a painting on the wall opposite her, the one that had been crooked when she arrived. Efram had obviously straightened it while she was in the bathroom. He told her it was by a Puerto Rican artist. *Heartsease*, it was called and showed two lovers embracing. The couple leaned against a dusty table in a rundown desert village. The woman's shirt was open, and one of the man's hands clutched her breast. The other held her tightly against him while he kissed her deeply. They both wore tight jeans that, to Joy, looked hot and uncomfortable. The woman's knees were bent, her legs open, and he between them. The dirt and sweat clinging to their bodies seemed to drift off the painting. Joy was beginning to feel warm and uncomfortable as well, so she turned her attention to the cool, flowing fern that hung beside the painting.

"Efram, doesn't that fern seem out of place next to that painting?" she decided to ask.

Efram came out of his trance. He was always oblivious to his surroundings when he worked. Glancing up, he saw the fern she referred to. "It gets a lot of light there." Efram sucked on his cheek. "Never thought of it being out of place. Besides, the lovers need a place to hide when they get going." He chuckled and winked.

"I don't like that painting, and I don't want to stare at it every day."

"Not moving it."

"Can we take a break?"

"We just started!"

"My neck hurts."

"It's been – what – ten minutes, Joy."

Efram frowned and reluctantly got up. Joy rolled her neck, popping it. He cringed at the sound.

"You get stiff that easily, this is gonna take awhile," he said, sitting beside her and massaging her shoulders. "Why don't you lie down?" Looking up at him, she decided to trust him and lay face down on the window seat. Efram climbed on top of her and straddled her back. His hands stroked her, causing her to bury her face in the cushions.

"Take off your clothes," he whispered in her ear, almost giggling.

Joy made a face. "I don't think so."

"That usually works with my other models."

"I'm not a bimbo."

"Touché. But Joy, that's the only way for me to give you a proper massage."

"I'm sure your magic fingers will penetrate through the fabric," she answered, lost in the thought of undressing before him.

"That's what I hope."

He pushed her hair to one side and began massaging her neck and shoulders. His fingertips were soft, but she could feel the rough dry paint on his hands. His long fingers dug into the sides of her neck, tickling her just a little. She let out a small moan, which embarrassed her. She kept her eyes closed, and her vocal cords still, as Efram began to hum. He made deep pinches in her back, molding her skin like putty.

After running the course of her back, he stroked her legs, which startled her. She kept very still, but alert, wondering now if she should trust him, hoping that she shouldn't. Efram shifted and sat beside her. He caressed her ankles and her feet as slowly as honey sliding across a plate. As his fingertips massaged her, his hands wanted to wander farther into her body, as deep as he could, until he felt not only the warmth of her insides but her dreams, her past lives, and her future.

"Roll over," he commanded.

When she did, the loose fabric almost revealed too much of her flesh, but she pulled it closed. Efram pretended not to notice. He ran his hands up and down her legs, then rubbed her arms, leaning over and letting his breath, scented with raspberry tea, breeze her cheeks. Joy shivered like on an autumn afternoon. She kept her eyes closed, but Efram read her like a psychic by listening to her shallow breathing, feeling the chill bumps on her skin, and watching the movement under her eyelids. Her lashes fluttered like a piece of paper caught in a breeze.

Efram stopped, nudging Joy back from bliss, knowing she would see the painting of the two lovers differently before long.

Chapter 12

Lemon Balm

The rain and thunder crashed like a head-on collision. Efram was busy setting out his art supplies when Joy bounded through the door, dripping wet and shaking herself dry like an alley cat. Efram curled up his lip when he glanced over his shoulder and saw her. "What happened to you?" he asked. Joy rolled her eyes and hurried to the bathroom to towel off.

"Don't you have an umbrella? It's an investment you should make," Efram yelled to her, arranging his brushes. One of them kept rolling off his small work table, and instead of moving it to another side, he snapped it in half.

"Like he couldn't have picked me up today," Joy muttered to herself as she slipped out of her wet Calvin & Hobbes T-shirt and cut-off shorts. "Do you have a hair dryer?" she hollered. Efram yelled the answer and she found it, not where he said, but under a towel instead.

Emerging from the bathroom, hair dried and wearing her goddess outfit, Joy flung a wet towel at Efram. She expected a wisecrack, but got a towel in the face in return.

By ruining his light, the rainstorm had put Efram on edge, but it was an early-morning phone call from Alana that had really unnerved him. When he awoke to hear her voice on the other end, he flung the phone down, but he couldn't go back to sleep. Alana's face kept popping into his pre-sleep thoughts. She was supposed to have left Wenton. There was no way he would ever do an art show for her just to save her allegedly drug-free self. She could die for all Efram cared. He surely didn't care if she was broke.

Now, he feared another visit. And with the storm as well, he was reluctant to paint, feeling too much anger. He was thinking about calling off the session.

While Joy went to the kitchen for a snack, Efram pulled out the painting in progress. It was pushed into a corner to keep Joy from seeing it; he hated anyone to see his work before it was complete. So far, so good, he thought, and a smile slid over his face. "You're a pretty good little artist, Efram T. Corbet," he told himself. Although the portrait was far from finished, he could see the work emerging as one of his best. He wouldn't rush it, though. He never did. He always left room for the work itself to have an opinion. There was no sense in throwing colors on canvas without a narrator to guide him. This time, he felt his guide was a pair of hands gliding over a woman's body for the first time, touching her, playing her like an instrument. She was wine and he was drinking her in, becoming fiercely intoxicated and giddy with her beauty. He picked up the broken brush and pushed the two ends together.

Efram's fantasies raced as he stared at the raindrops sliding down the windowpane. He heard Joy clinking dishes and the patter of her feet, so he quickly pushed the painting into the corner. As she returned to the living room, carrying a glass of tea and a plate of nacho cheese Doritos with a dab of sour cream on the side, her gown flowed at her feet with each step, like an angel's.

"If you spill that on your outfit ... "

"Ooooh, I'm really scared," Joy said and sat down on the window seat.

"Why don't you just eat Cheetos? Then you could get even *more* cheese on your fingertips. You want to be immortalized with orange fingers?"

"You're an artist. Work around it."

Efram smiled appreciatively at Joy's remark, as thunder rocked the house. Joy moved to the couch, scared of lightning coming through the window. Efram, on the other hand, ready to squeeze her likeness from his brush and smear it on canvas, opened the window seat and pulled out a roll of tape. He taped the two ends of the paintbrush together and sat down on the stool.

"Storms make me testy, but I'm ready if you are," he said to Joy as she crammed two chips into her mouth at once. "Hungry?" he asked. Joy smiled. "I was gonna work an hour, then have some lunch." Munching on the chips, Joy nodded. Feeling his own stomach growl, Efram gave up and went to the kitchen to make avocado and bean sprout sandwiches. "All right, you cow," he said.

After lunch, Joy returned to her all-too-familiar window seat. Only day two, and the seat was like home. Efram sat down beside her and arranged her hair. The storm was growing worse. Trees, rocking like a child's wooden horse, flicked away leaves like confetti. Water sloshed up and down the driveway. Efram's car was a mere blur. At school, Joy had heard rumors of tornadoes in the southern part of the state, so Efram turned on the radio, which ironically was playing Madonna's *Rain*.

"I guess the radio guy's trying to be funny," he said. Efram moved a piece of hair behind Joy's ear, then ran his hand under her chin and kissed her. It made her blush and he liked the color. "Let's get started," he said and patted her cheek.

The cool window was fogged over with her breath and she wiped it to peek outside. The warmth from his lips was still present. She leaned back, getting into position for Efram. As she did, she could feel the crick in her neck waiting for her any minute. By break time, it would have total control of her body.

Even with the storm, it was still hot, and a bead of sweat slipped down Joy's chest just as Efram let the color drip down the canvas to become her body. His brush went up and down the eager canvas as his hands did when he gave Joy a massage. Her eyes followed his strokes; a little shiver went through her as he molded, touched, and recreated her. Again, she felt naked, while Efram let the paintbrush have its way with her. He toyed with the folds of Joy's gown with delicate strokes. So many of them, he thought. He let them flow like the rain cascading on the window behind her.

Thunder hit the house like a bomb, causing Efram to lose control of his brush and smear his work. "Dammit!" he cried and tried to conceal it.

"Is it okay? I saw your hand jerk," Joy asked, using the diversion to scratch her nose.

He muttered that it was fine, not telling Joy that he had created a large white smudge across her face.

After spending an hour concealing his mistake, he sighed and placed his palette on the small table beside him. "Break," he said. They both stretched, and Efram turned up the radio. Throughout the hour, the weather reports had kept interrupting the music. It seemed the storm was growing like ice crystals on a cold windowpane. If the reports were accurate, the worst was yet to come. The wind made a harsh sound, causing Mr. Boogie to whimper and pace back and forth. A weather bulletin announced that a tornado and severe thunderstorm warning was in effect. Certain counties had been advised to take cover. Joy leaned on Efram's shoulder as they listened to the report.

"What'dya say to a nice run through the rain?" Efram suggested, rubbing her back.

Joy shook her head. "Efram, this is the South. Did you forget? Tornadoes are serious business here." She pulled back the curtain.

"I have a storm shelter out back," he said. She nodded and told him she had played dungeon in it as a child. He remembered the one his family had back in Arkansas. Never once did they use it, but it was always serious business to his father. Efram was not allowed to play in it. His father told him stories of whole houses being blown away. This never scared Efram from the rain, but it did make him feel claustrophobic about storm shelters. He just knew that their house would land on top of the shelter and trap them inside.

Joy punched him in the gut and said, "So, what's for dessert?"

"Left-over lemon pie from yesterday."

Joy rubbed her belly. "Sounds peachy."

"No, lemony. Peach pie tomorrow." He chuckled. Joy rolled her eyes.

While Efram was in the kitchen, Joy called Katie to say she was all right. Her family still had no idea she was with Efram, and she was quite proud of the deception. She loved that it made her feel sneaky, but she did not feel good that Efram was unaware that she had to deceive her family to be with him.

The reception on the phone was terrible, but she heard Katie say hello through the static. "It's Joy. Can you hear me?" Joy barely heard a static-covered affirmative. "Are you all right? Is everything ... " The line cut out then quickly came back, still covered in static. "I'm over at a friend's." Katie asked who she was with; Joy used the static to her advantage when Efram came in and yelled, "Hey, guess what? I got artificial weenies! That Brooke's guy ordered 'em for me." Realizing she was on the phone, he covered his mouth and moonwalked back into the kitchen.

"Who was that, Joy?" Katie asked.

"I can't hear you, Katie. I gotta go." She hung up and went to the kitchen.

"What was that about artificial weenies? Those kind of devices are illegal in this county," she said, tapping her foot and grinning.

He raised an eyebrow. "Dirty mind." He pointed to the living room. "Sorry, I didn't know you were on the phone."

"S'all right. I told them I was safe with a friend."

"But not with me?"

"You're a friend." Joy sat down at the kitchen table and played with the place mat. "Artificial weenies?"

"Made from soy."

"I'll have one of those weenies."

Efram raised his eyebrows and said, "I thought you wanted dessert?"

She shrugged. "Both are good."

"You're going to lose that girlish figure if you keep eating like this."

"Not worried."

Efram looked her up and down. "Yeah. I'd say you still have a few good years left in you." He winked and Joy blushed.

◌৪৪১

After their snack, the rain didn't let up; the drops hit the window next to Joy like BBs being shot from a machine gun. The wind hissed like a cat being chased by a mad dog, and the electricity flickered as if signaling disaster. Efram painted until the room grew gloomy. Although it was far from dusk, it was already very dark outside. Efram flipped on a few lights and continued to paint.

Joy stretched. "Enough for today?"

Before he could answer, a limb smashed against the window then crashed to the ground. Joy screamed and jumped up.

"Enough for today," he said. "We should go to the shelter."

Joy changed clothes. Fortunately, only the waistband of her shorts was still damp. As she slipped on her sandals, the lights went out for good. Efram cursed and paint cans rattled as he kicked his way around the living room. He fumbled through a drawer for a flashlight. When he found it, he flipped the light on and off like a child. As Joy stepped out of the bathroom, he flashed it towards her, hitting her in the face. She covered her eyes and he pointed the beam at her feet. Then, with Mr. Boogie in one arm and Joy following, he threw open the back door. Like maniacs, they ran screaming to the shelter.

The wind nearly knocked them down, and the rain felt like needles hooked to a jackhammer. As they reached the shelter, they realized it was hail. Joy slipped on the mixture of freshly mowed grass and mud. Efram helped her up and yanked open the heavy cement door. After being nearly shoved inside, Joy held on to the railing and cautiously moved down the steps. Efram held the flashlight on her until she reached the bottom, then he pulled the door closed. It clanked shut like a prison door. Mr. Boogie leaped from Efram's grip, and they both shook off the water – the dog twisting his body; Efram ruffling his hair. With the beam from the flashlight, Efram roamed the room looking for the lantern. Finding it on a warped board that posed as a shelf, he lit it, then turned to Joy, who sat shivering on a small roll-away bed. She was a stunning contrast to the cold, dark gray walls.

Efram pulled down some towels from another shelf and handed one to her. "Good thing I stocked this place, or we'd be up a shit creek," he said, drying his face.

"Or in a creek, the way this is coming down," Joy muttered, attacking her wet hair with the towel. Efram laughed. Like him, she always knew how to turn a serious moment into a lighthearted one.

The hail banged on the door as if it wanted refuge from the storm as well. Mr. Boogie howled. "Gosh, he sounds awful," Joy said, frowning. Efram picked up the dog, set him in his lap, and toweled him dry. He calmed down as Efram stroked him. Joy reached over to pet the little dog and discovered it had a calming effect on her, too. She had always wanted a dog, but Emily was allergic. They had once had a dog, a poodle Katie found lapping water in a nearby pond. It had been the Baxter pet only a few hours when Emily broke out in a rash. The dog was given to a neighbor, but Katie and Joy were too upset to go visit a dog that didn't belong to them anymore.

Efram placed Mr. Boogie on the bed and turned on the radio. It blasted forth warnings and unwelcome promises of more to come. Joy's thoughts turned to her family. They didn't have a storm shelter at home, and she wondered what Katie would do for cover. She hoped her mother and Emily had places to go at work. "I hope my family is all right," she said.

Efram rubbed her back. "Of course they are, Joy. Don't worry." He took her hand and made her lean against him. She was still shivering, so he pulled an army blanket around her. Rocking her in his arms made him think of the time he as a child had decided to dance naked in the rain. His father had arrived home to see Efram sloshing around. He grabbed Efram's arm, pulled him up the steps, and whipped him on the porch. Efram's mother cuddled him when he walked into the house, naked and humiliated.

Something rapped on the door, and Efram nearly got up to answer it. He remembered a story about monsters banging on the door, but decided against telling it to Joy. They sat in silence and listened to the radio, which was becoming immersed in static faster than the rain hitting the ground.

The storm went on for over an hour. Then silence. Efram looked at Joy. They sat there for a few minutes before Efram got up to open the door. "Joy, come look at this." The sky was yellow and the trees were still as the dead. She tugged at Efram and he closed the door. The radio issued a stern warning: "Take cover now!" The station went silent. The roar of the town siren could be heard through the cement walls. The nearby church bells rang, and Joy buried her face in Efram's chest. Although she'd lived through warning after warning, this was her very first tornado. Efram pretended to be unafraid but was just as inexperienced.

In the distance, they heard a faint noise, like an ocean liner running aground, the captain tugging on the horn with a granite-filled arm. It grew louder and louder. Mr. Boogie jumped from the bed and ran in circles. Efram told Joy to lie down on the bed, and he nonchalantly climbed on top of her, protecting her, he thought, in case the shelter wasn't strong enough. Though not oblivious to her warm belly, he could think only of his childhood fear of a collapsing house.

The bolt on the door rattled and Joy screamed. The shelter shook slightly, and to her it felt like an earthquake. Objects crashed against the door, and the wind swished overhead. Joy thought the sound could burst an eardrum, but it lasted only a few seconds. Then, again, silence.

They stayed still for several minutes. The rain started to patter lightly on the roof, and the radio popped back on. The station confirmed that a tornado had touched down. Joy pushed Efram off her and rolled over on her stomach, letting her hand scrape the floor. Mr. Boogie, who had spent the ordeal under the bed, greeted her palm with a wet lick.

Efram got up to open the door, only to be stopped by a radio announcement. The worst of the storm was not over. Another front was moving through with heavy winds, possible tornadoes, and hail. Joy sighed and rolled onto her back. Power and telephone lines were down as well, causing fires all over town. Efram opened the door a crack to make sure they weren't trapped and to see if his house was still standing. It was.

∞

Efram's flashlight highlighted the destruction and the rain that pitter-pattered on the roof. A few windows were broken and the floor was covered in glass, vines, and twigs. The kitchen utensils were in disarray. The curtain rods dangled lifelessly from the wall, and the curtains lay in sodden heaps. Water was everywhere. The roses Efram had used in Joy's painting were scattered about, torn and mangled. His stool was overturned and his paint cans pushed against the wall. He had safely stored the painting of Joy in the hall closet and it remained there, unharmed. Flashing the light out of a broken window, Efram saw that his car was on its side.

"It's not so bad, Ef," Joy told him. She was holding on to the back of his shirt as they tried to maneuver through the debris.

"Yeah, just a few broken windows. It's no problem. Hope the car is okay. Let's go push it over," he said and grabbed her arm. Joy shook her head, but he continued to drag her back into the rain.

"Efram ... we shouldn't be out in this."

The porch swing was a twisted mess and Efram yanked it back into place. He carefully surveyed the ground before walking down the steps. The rain began to fall harder, and Efram pulled Joy along towards his car. The beam from the flashlight caught a downed power line and Efram halted. They both stepped over it and ran to the car.

The car was covered in mud, the hood torn and smashed. Efram spun a tire, letting his fingers run along the treads. "Come on, let's get around it. We can push it back," he said. Efram stood near the hood and Joy near the back. They pushed like two workmen, and the car loudly toppled over. They both jumped back and stared at it. Efram peered inside and then at his surroundings.

"I don't think it's safe for you to go home," he told her.

"You think I should stay here? Stay the night?" Joy asked, already knowing his reply and fearing it.

"The storm isn't over. With power lines down and my car a mess, it's not a good idea to drive, and I don't think you should walk. We better get back inside," he said.

"Yeah," she replied and pushed wet strands of hair from her face. She never anticipated staying the night with Efram. Now she had to take a big leap in trusting him.

Back inside the house, she tried the phone and found it was dead.

Efram rubbed her shoulders. "Joy, you told them earlier that you were at a friend's, so they know you're safe. I'm sure they're fine, too."

She nodded and chewed her lip.

Mr. Boogie wagged his tail when they walked in the shelter. Efram threw him a dog biscuit, which he had picked up in the house on the way back, along with dry clothes. The radio was broadcasting on-the-scene destruction reports. Many homes had been destroyed, and Efram felt lucky. He switched the radio off, fearing the reports would worry Joy about her home and her family.

Joy wrapped her arms around herself and began to think of every possible disaster that could have hit them.

Efram smiled and patted her head. "I'm sure your family is fine, Joy. Don't worry."

"Yeah, I guess so."

"Here, put on my pajama bottoms and this T-shirt. You look cold. This will warm you up," he said, handing her the dry clothes. "I'll turn around. I won't peek."

Quickly, Joy slipped out of her wet clothes and into the warm flannel of Efram's pajamas. She pulled the drawstring as tight as she could. Turning around, she caught sight of Efram's bare back as a fresh T-shirt slid over his body. She looked away and sat down to roll up the pajama legs.

"Comfy?" Efram asked, taking a seat beside her. She shrugged.

Efram found more blankets on a shelf that carried his supplies: a first-aid kit, nonperishable foods, and batteries. He shook a can of peanuts and asked Joy if she wanted any, then opened the can anyway and handed it to her. Mr. Boogie curled up beside her and sniffed the can. Efram nudged them both off the bed and spread the blankets over it. "Which side do you want, Joy? Left or right? Dog gets the center."

"Um," she answered through a mouthful of cashews. "I'm not sure about ... "

"I'm not going to do anything, Joy. Don't you trust me?"

She blushed. "No. I mean, yes, I trust you. Left is fine. Whatever."

"Geez. It's not like I planned it. You wanna try to venture out in this weather?"

"It's fine! Really."

"Testy." Efram put his hand to his chin and looked around. "Only have one pillow," he said. "We'll have to share." He reached up on the shelf again and pulled down a deck of cards. "Wanna play?" Joy nodded. A game of poker would be perfect for a night that was already such a gamble.

Efram crawled into the bed. Mr. Boogie followed, snuggling in the middle. Efram put his arm around the dog while Joy situated herself under the covers. Then he handed her the cards and told her to shuffle.

Later, when Efram owned Joy's entire arrowhead collection, her one designer gown, and her Motown boxed set, they stopped playing. Efram, the spoiled winner, threw his arms up in victory. "You suck at this game," he said.

Joy shook her head, suggesting a game of Go Fish. Efram scoffed.

"When I'm on such a winning streak?"

"Count me out then."

He took the cards and began to organize them by suit.

"What are you doing?" Joy lay down and pulled the covers tighter. The wind was still wailing and the rain still pounded on the roof.

"Putting the cards away," Efram explained.

"Now *that* is anal."

The digital clock blinked to eight o'clock. "So, you want to do something else?" Efram asked.

Joy shrugged. "What?"

"I don't know." Efram got up to put away the cards. The bed bounced up and down like a cheap water bed. He stood over her, staring at her hair, curled from being damp. She looked beautiful. "You sleepy?" he asked.

"Not really."

Efram got back into bed and rolled over on his side, facing her, while Joy stared at the ceiling. This was the most awkward moment she'd had since her first date at fifteen. What was she supposed to do? Tell him her feelings? Kiss him good night? She could feel Mr. Boogie pushing against her. The little dog buried his face in Efram's neck, tickling him with his breath. Efram giggled and pushed him away.

The lantern flickered and made shadows dance on the walls. "That one looks like a giant lemon," Efram said.

Joy snorted.

"It does," he insisted. He had a craving for herb tea made with lemon balm. Whenever he had trouble sleeping or felt tense, he fixed that tea. It calmed him down quickly. Being alone with Joy in bed, made him uneasy. If it had been any other woman, he would know what to do. They would have sex.

"I've never met anyone like you," he said.

Joy turned to face him. "In what way?"

"Innocent."

"I'm not innocent."

He chuckled and rolled over. "You are."

Before long, they both drifted off to sleep, although Joy stayed awake long after Efram. She enjoyed the soft splashes of an ending rainstorm and the incoherent mumbles from Efram's dreams. Each time his arm flung over her body and knocked her in the face, she pushed it back, then hoped he'd do it again. As she fluttered in and out of her own dreams, Efram yanked the covers away from her. This gave her an excuse to snuggle closer. The dog, through the course of the night, moved to the foot of the bed for fear of being crushed by two dreaming humans.

~ ~ ~

Efram was outside cleaning his car with the garden hose when Joy awoke. She put on her own clothes and stepped outside to see Mr. Boogie on his leash, chained to a tree in the yard. Joy tickled his chin and told him, "Can't play in the yard until it's safe, little guy." She gave him a final pat on the head and hurried toward Efram. The car was covered in mud and twigs. Efram was reaching inside to wipe the seat when Joy came up behind him and tugged on his shirt.

"Hey, you're up, sleepyhead. So, what do you think? It's not so bad, eh?" he asked her, pointing to the car's interior.

"Nothing a little Armor All can't fix. Does she run?" Joy asked, slipping her hands in her back pockets.

"Is my car a girl?"

"Huh?"

"Never mind." Efram climbed in and motioned for Joy to do the same. The seats were wet and she scooted down to the edge of hers. Efram inserted the key and the car roared to a start.

"Pretty good for a car that was tipped over, don't ya think?" he asked. The car sounded fine, but Efram was worried about the scuffs to the passenger's side and the smashed hood. "I'll have to find a body shop that can knock out the kinks, but I think it'll be okay. You want me to drive you home?" Joy hesitated.

"You want to walk? I imagine it's a mess out there," he said. "I'll drive you."

Reluctantly, she nodded. Joy went into Efram's house to find her book bag and discovered the place was a mess. The sunlight made it look like nature had a wild party in Efram's living room. Joy tried the phone but it was dead; the power was still out. She stepped over books and broken glass to get to the bathroom, where her purse still sat near the sink, untouched by nature's hand.

"It's a mess in there," Efram yelled to her as she came out. Joy nodded and ran to his car.

"I'll help you straighten up later."

"I'll be fine."

Downed power lines had made some of the streets impassable, but the drive to Joy's house was clear. The fallen lines were the least of her worries. As she arrived home, her mother peered through the kitchen window when she heard Efram's car pull into the driveway. He grinned and waved to her. Joy climbed out of the car.

"Bye, Efram. House looks fine," she said and went indoors. Efram watched her, then peeled away.

Joy was ready for a question-and-answer session, but was happy that her family was safe and their house undamaged. Her two sisters were at the table eating pancakes. Emily jumped up and hugged her as soon as she entered.

"Joy! We were so worried!" Emily exclaimed. She looked Joy over. "Who did you stay with? Katie couldn't make it out on the phone last night."

Beverly frowned and threw down the dish towel she had been wringing in her hands all morning. She shook her finger at Joy. "Who was that bringing you home?"

"My friend," Joy said and took a seat at the table.

Beverly nodded and put one hand on her hip. "Friend huh? That's Efram Corbet. Since when is he your friend?"

"The artist guy?" asked Katie. "Sweet! This is getting good!" Katie chewed slowly, waiting for Joy's reply.

Joy rolled her eyes. "I was walking home, and he picked me

up. He's nice. He's brought me home before," Joy said, but had an inkling her lie was not going to hold up.

Katie's eyes widened. "You rode in the car?"

"Yes, the Porsche. It's no big deal."

"I see," Beverly replied, chewing on her bottom lip.

"Why do you care?"

"It doesn't look nice," Emily said calmly. "He's, you know ... "

"Since it matters so much, he's only *part* black," Joy said and stood up. "Don't you people have places to go?"

"Shit! I'm gonna be late!" Emily exclaimed, dropping her fork, leaving her pancakes unfinished. Katie scooped up the uneaten food as Emily ran out with a wave.

"This has nothing to do with the color of his skin," Beverly responded after waving to Emily.

"Right. What is it then? I have to get to class."

"Classes were cancelled," Katie said. "Unfortunately, the Dairy Hut is open. Can you believe that shit?" She rolled her eyes.

"Katie, language!" Beverly said, pacing the room. "How do you know him? How did you meet him?"

"It's personal. I have the right to my privacy."

"Are you seeing him?"

"Sorta."

"Tender!" Katie yelled and smacked her palm against the table top.

Beverly pushed her hair behind her ear then rubbed the back of her neck. "He's too old for you, too worldly. You're too young to understand."

"Oh please!" Joy responded and stormed out of the room. Her mother followed.

"Joy, we aren't finished."

"We are."

"Joy Marie Baxter!"

Joy sighed and rested her head against the wall. "I'm sorry, Mother, but I'm going to see him. I have a contractual obligation to him."

"What?"

"He's painting my portrait. He's an artist, you know."
"Good lord. Not nude?"

"Fully clothed," Joy responded, not mentioning the material that was so sheer it was possible to see her breasts in the right light.

Chapter 13

Calamint

With the table set and the dinner ready, Joy paced the floor, pinching her bottom lip with her fingers as she always did when she got too nervous. The family sat, pretty as a portrait in a photographer's studio, waiting to meet Efram T. Corbet, who was late for Sunday lunch. Katie tapped her foot and wriggled in her loose-fitting pink dress, while Emily stirred butter into the peas and smacked her gum. Beverly twirled the phone cord and looked like she was listening for it to ring – maybe it would be Efram, cancelling.

Joy was still amazed that she had convinced her mother to invite Efram to lunch. After much arguing, Joy had said, "You can't judge him if you don't know him." Beverly had relented, thinking Joy might not go for the suggestion, and said, "Fine. Invite him over for lunch on Sunday." Joy had felt victorious until her mother realized Joy had lied about working at Sears, too. That information had caused another whirl of arguments.

Hearing the whir of a car engine outside, Joy stopped pacing and peeked out the window. "He's here," she announced, rubbing her palms together. Accidentally, Beverly tipped over a flower vase; the neatly arranged collection of wild flowers spilled over the counter. A sprig of baby's breath slipped to the floor. Without realizing it, Beverly kicked it under the table as she reorganized the flowers in the vase.

Emily replaced the lid on the peas, and Katie muttered a "finally" and ran to open the door. Joy rushed after her, but she did not beat Katie to the door. Efram stood there with a wide grin.

"Hi, you must be Katie. I'm sorry I'm late, but I stopped off for Evian," Efram said and held out his hand. Beverly and Emily came to the door. As if he were a con man come to sell defunct vacuum cleaners, they stared at him.

"Ef!" exclaimed Joy. "You made it! Come in." She reached around Katie, seized Efram's arm, and pulled him inside. Her family quickly scrambled out of his way, but continued to look him over.

Efram handed Beverly the Evian and then put his hands on his hips. "Nice place you got here," he remarked. Beverly nodded and motioned for him to sit down. Joy sat beside him on the couch, crossed her legs, and patted his shoulder. Efram sighed softly. "Something sure smells good, ma'am," he said, trying to remember some of his Southern charm. "You must be a great cook."

"Actually, you have Emily to thank. She does a lot of the cooking around here," said Beverly, tersely.

"I see. What will our taste buds be feasting on, Emily?" Efram asked, as polite as he could stand. Years of hobnobbing with socialites and celebrities made him accustomed to phoney banter.

"Fried chicken, mashed potatoes, peas, homemade rolls, and coconut cake. Could I get you something to drink?" Emily replied. "I'm sure the, um, water you brought is lovely."

Efram winked. "Actually, this sounds like a meal fit for iced tea, if it's not too much trouble."

Emily hurried to the kitchen with Katie following, anxious to gossip. Beverly shook her head and turned to Efram. "So, Joy tells me you're painting her portrait."

Joy sighed. "Must we discuss this now, Mother?"

"It's okay, Joy. Yes, ma'am. Joy told me you were worried about it, but it's totally harmless. I'm a professional and it's always nice to see a fresh face. I have her posed on my window seat. She's wearing a white gown, kind of like a Greek goddess."

Beverly nodded. "Oh."

"I have a portfolio in the car, if you'd like to see."

"No nudity?"

Efram smiled. "No, ma'am. No nudity."

Emily and Katie came back with the tea. Efram took a sip and smiled. "Are we ready for the salad?" Emily asked everyone. Katie skipped back to the kitchen, while Beverly got up from her seat and motioned for Efram and Joy to join them.

Efram rubbed Joy's back as they walked to the kitchen. He whispered, "Did I pass?"

"Too early to tell," she responded quietly.

The table was neatly arranged with place settings for five people. The napkins were red-and-white checkerboard like something from a picnic basket. The tablecloth, a starched white linen, was a perfect frame for the white plates decorated with a red rose pattern. The pattern made Efram feel nostalgic. He ran his fingers over the little raised petals and took a deep breath, smiling to himself as he remembered the time he autographed his mother's tablecloth with red crayon. Next to his signature, he drew the rose pattern of her dinner plates. When she discovered what he had done, instead of scolding him, she remarked about how lovely it was. His father peered from behind the sports section and, being preoccupied with the Cowboys, only nodded his head. The next day his mother cut out the spot and framed it. Now, sitting at a family table in Wenton, Efram had the urge to do it again.

"Efram, would you like Thousand Island, ranch, or Italian dressing?" Emily asked.

"Do you have any balsamic vinegar?"

Emily shook her head and repeated. "We have Thousand Island, ranch, and Italian."

Katie chuckled under her breath, and Joy kicked Efram under the table. "Just pick one," Joy told him.

Efram chose ranch, and Emily scooped out a huge portion of salad into everyone's bowl. Efram waited for Emily to pour a glass of tea for everyone before even touching a utensil. After she sat down and they all began to eat, Efram picked up his salad fork.

They ate quietly, only discussing the tornado – how the new Wal-Mart was destroyed, who had lost what, and the miraculous-survival stories people were telling in town. Efram, who knew no one else in Wenton, only nodded or raised his eyebrows when they brought up long-time family friends who had escaped destruction or injury.

"So, how is the damage to your home?" Emily asked.

Efram put down his fork. "Well, it wasn't so bad, as I'm sure Joy told you, but bad enough to keep grubby workmen in my house and me out. I've been at a hotel and it's driving me nuts, but I can't very well live without windows. There was a lot of water damage in the kitchen, so I had to put in some new flooring."

"You're lucky. Some homes were demolished," Beverly said.

"Yeah, this girl at the Dairy Hut, her house is gone. Just ripped apart. Creepy," Katie said with her mouth full.

"Joy told me you worked there. How do you like it? I bet you get all the malts you can drink."

"It sucks."

"Katie, language," Beverly scolded.

"I would rather have the whole summer off, but I like the money. It's the hours that stink."

Efram grinned. "What grade're ya gonna be in this fall?" His Southern accent was returning.

"Tenth. Hey, can I ride in your Porsche later?"

"Maybe later." Efram said with a smile. "Joy told me you really liked it."

"Sweet!"

"Do you like the salad?" Emily asked Efram.

Before he could respond, Katie added, "There aren't any flowers in it. You really eat flowers?"

"Katie!" Beverly admonished her again. "Where are your manners today?"

Efram laughed. "Yes. Yes, I do, and they're quite good. Not just any kind of flower. Some you can't eat. Like the Venus flytrap. It eats you."

They all laughed. Joy gave a sigh of relief; Efram always knew how to get the reaction he wanted. "Do you want some more tea?" Joy asked and dabbed her face with her napkin before getting up to pour him a glass.

The rest of the meal went smoothly. By the time Beverly served dessert, they were asking about Efram's upbringing. He told them about his parents, about growing up in Arkansas, his life in New York, and his work. This seemed to impress them and they pursued nothing further. Mostly, he thought, because they did not know there was more to find out. Joy, however, knew they were being polite.

Efram stayed for coffee and a round of Trivial Pursuit in the living room, which caused Katie to become bored and spend the rest of the evening on the phone. "She doesn't like this game much," Beverly explained.

Joy whispered to Efram, "She's just stupid, really."

After an hour of play, everyone got bored, and they put the game away. Katie returned and headed for the kitchen. When she walked back into the living room holding a glass of wine, Beverly scolded her. "Since when do you drink wine, young lady? Put that away."

Joy reacted like a mother seeing her child about to walk in front of a moving car. "You can't have that! Your baby!" Joy grimaced, realizing she had given up Katie's secret.

As the realization of what Joy had said hit everyone in the room, like a baseball about to fly over the fence, there was silence. Then Katie slammed the glass against the wall. Slivers of thin glass flew into the air and fell on the carpet like bits of a feather.

"Katie!" Beverly cried. "Baby?"

"You stupid bitch!" Katie yelled at Joy. "I told you not to tell, but you just couldn't hold back!" She ran into the hallway away from the prying.

Joy tried to explain. "I didn't mean to. It was an accident, Katie!"

"You knew?" Emily exclaimed.

Beverly drew a deep breath like a sailor breathing in the stench of an unfriendly harbor.

"I should go," Efram said and got up.

"I'm outta here, too," Joy replied and took Efram by the arm.

"Katie! Katherine! Come back here!" Beverly called, ignoring Efram and Joy's departure. Emily sat motionless, stunned at what had happened.

Outside on the porch with his hands in his pockets, Efram

glanced at Joy, not sure what to say.

"Sorry about that," Joy said, pointing at the door with her thumb.

"I understand. It's cool. You sure you shouldn't stay?"

"I don't want to."

"I'm heading back to my little hotel room. Or, the closet, as I have affectionately nicknamed it. You want to come?"

Joy nodded. They walked to Efram's car and got in. As Efram buckled his seat belt, he asked, "So why didn't you tell me about Katie?"

"Tell you? Why would you care?"

He shrugged. "I get nosy every so often."

"I didn't feel it was important to you."

"I want to know what's going on in your life."

Joy felt her skin flush. He cared about her. She was embarking on her last week of summer session one, still amazed that the seven weeks were almost up; however, her finals were the last thing on her mind. Joy struggled with the decision whether to go to school in San Antonio in the coming spring. She had received a letter from the archeology professor asking if she was going to enroll and go on the archeological dig. The situation with her family was no longer an issue. With Katie's baby coming, she wanted to get out, but she didn't want to leave Efram.

Although still dented and scratched, the car engine showed no signs of being the victim of a recent storm, and Efram pulled out of the driveway onto the street.

"I have some things to tell you," he said. Joy kept staring out the window, but did not ignore his remark.

⊂≳⥰⊃

At the Marriott, Efram stopped at the vending machine for a Clark bar and a bag of pork rinds. He explained to Joy that Mr. Boogie was contraband at the hotel, and the pork rinds were a little treat for his canine friend, who could only go out for walks at night.

"Is the room okay? You didn't say much when I called Wednesday," Joy asked, dropping three quarters into the machine for a bag of M&Ms.

"It'll do. I'll be glad when I can leave, of course."

They walked down the long hallway until they reached room 333. Mr. Boogie leaped from the couch and greeted them both with a wag of his tail.

"How do you keep the maid from finding him?"

"I got it all worked out." Efram opened the bag of pork rinds and put them in the dog's bowl. The dog ate the treats like he was famished. "I'm here most of the time, and when I'm not, I put out the Do Not Disturb sign. I call the housekeeper at night to bring up towels. I can clean for myself."

"You're gonna get caught." Joy took a seat on the couch and opened the M&Ms. She noticed the room smelled heavily of calamint potpourri. "This room smells like catnip. Maybe you aren't the only one to have snuck a pet in here."

"Probably not, but the calamint is my doing. Catnip in potpourri is a mood elevator for people. Did you know that? It can be used as a pain reliever, as well."

"Your knowledge of herbs and plants is quite impressive."

"Witch doctor, remember?"

"Right. Witch doctor from Arkansas." She popped a few M&Ms into her mouth, then asked, "So, what do you have to tell me?"

Efram sat down beside her. He had so much to expunge and knew Joy would listen; however, he hated to bring up old wounds. His troubles with Alana felt like sores that would never fully heal. If anyone could make it feel better, he knew it would be Joy. Joy was like a mother's kiss – it always took away the pain. "I have this friend Alana, and I'm not sure if I've mentioned her to you or not."

A twinge of jealousy shot through Joy.

"She helped me out a lot in New York, gave me my start, and molded my career. I was grateful at first. She knows everything about the art world. I wanted to be successful. It was glamorous and fun. Unfortunately, she showed me the dark side too, and I was more than willing to fall into it. She turned me into a cliché. A famous artist on drugs and alcohol with too many women and too much money."

Joy blushed at the "too many women" remark.

Efram got up and paced the room. "After my parents died, I just snapped out of it. I mean, I was getting there, you know. I knew things weren't good. My life was about money, parties. Then, my parents ... " His voice cracked.

"Efram, it's okay."

He sat down on the floor. "I got myself into rehab. Cleaned up. Alana was finally out of my life after being a bad part of it for a decade."

"A decade?" The green-eyed monster visited Joy again.

"I can't believe I let it go on that long either. It's been three years now, but I still see her at art shows and parties. It's hard to avoid her completely, since we're in the same business. I try to ignore her. She's one of the few people who can put me on edge."

He stood up, walked over to the couch, and sat down. He ruffled Mr. Boogie's fur. "Mr. Boogie liked to growl at her. They didn't get along too well."

"Dogs can always tell."

Efram laughed. "I should have adopted the little guy sooner!"

Even though it pained her with envy, she asked, "Was she your girlfriend, too?"

"I can't believe I loved her."

Loved her? Joy thought to herself, jealousy mode in full swing. So much of Efram's life was still a mystery to her.

"I guess she wasn't my girlfriend in the traditional sense. We both kept our options open, if you know what I mean."

Joy understood but felt so inexperienced compared to him.

"Anyway, that's all over now. Those feelings are long gone. In fact, I hate to admit it, but I think I even hate her. She caused me so much pain."

"I'm really sorry."

"It's okay. I just wanted to let you know about her, because she visited me here."

"Here? At the hotel?" Joy got up and walked around. She didn't want Efram to see the envious side of herself.

"She visited me at the house first. Wants me to do a show for her. Yeah, right. I tell her to buzz off."

Joy barely muttered a response. She nodded.

"Says she's cleaned up, but she's broke. Like I care. I guess she thought she'd keep harassing me. Fortunately, she left town, so maybe she got the hint."

Joy almost sighed but caught herself. She sat back down next to him and rubbed his leg like a wife consoling her husband. "I'm sorry, Ef. Don't let it get to you. She left, so it's okay now."

"Life is weird, because if you'd met me then, we wouldn't have become friends," he said, wrapping his arm around her.

"I guess things happen when they're supposed to," she said. "I'm glad we know each other now."

He pulled her close and kissed her, not passionately, but lightly on the forehead.

"All those years with Alana and I never felt for her what I feel for you."

"What do you feel?" she asked with a lump in her throat, knowing her jealousy had been in vain.

He climbed on top of her and kissed her neck, slowly opening her shirt and kissing her collar bone like it was the floor of heaven. "I love you," he whispered. Hearing the words roll out of his mouth was not a surprise. He knew them to be true. A shiver went up Joy's spine like a cat running the length of a railing. "Let's make love," he said, his voice now softer than a whisper, his tongue too busy to speak, concentrating on the hollow of her throat. As Joy was about to respond with a breathless yes, the housekeeper knocked on the door. Before they could get up, she entered and Mr. Boogie jumped on her, knocking her armload of towels to the ground – and Efram out of his room.

※

Back at the house, Joy climbed over the scattered lumber in Efram's yard. Since it was Sunday, the carpenters weren't around but the place was littered with their presence. She was careful not to step on nails and hammers. She picked up a power saw and placed it high up on the porch railing out of harms way for Mr. Boogie. The sunlight blinded her and she shielded her eyes with her hand. Efram loaded his luggage from the car and carried it inside. The heat reddened her face, but she knew her skin was still flushed from what had almost happened at the hotel. She tried to ignore Efram and clean up the yard, but he motioned for her to come inside.

"I'll make some tea," he hollered to her. She nodded.

Instinctively, Joy knew she loved him from the first moment she saw him. Without a doubt, she wanted to make love to him. As if picking up on her hesitation, Efram stepped out on the porch again. "Aren't you coming in? It's hot as hell out here."

Joy smiled and bounded up the steps. Mr. Boogie was curled up near a vent on the floor, enjoying the cool air sweeping through.

"It is hot," she said and took a seat in the kitchen. The new windows were trimmed with a pale yellow border. Given time to think about the prospect of making love to him, made her even more nervous. She grappled with something to talk about. "The new windows look nice."

"Yeah, I'm going to paint some little flowers around the border."

"This place is starting to look normal again. How much longer?"

Efram sat down. "Funny you should ask, because that's another thing I wanted to talk to you about. They'll be finished in a day or so with all the repairs, but there are some things I wanted to remodel before I moved in originally. I was too anxious to wait, so I never got around to it. I figured since I already have people working on the house, I'd go ahead and take care of it in one swoop."

"Makes sense, but this place isn't rundown or anything."

"Oh, I know, but the porch in the back needs to be redone, and I've thought about putting carpet in the bedroom. The bathroom plumbing is old. I'd prefer a more modern sink and tub. You have to admit the outside could stand a fresh paint job."

Joy didn't agree, but couldn't recall the last time it had been painted.

"I also need to put my car in the shop to knock out the dents and fix the hood."

The tea started to boil and Efram turned off the burner. Joy took out two glasses and filled them with ice as Efram poured the tea into a pitcher of cold water. He mixed in the sugar then dipped in the spoon to taste. "Perfect!" he said with a smile. Efram poured the tea into the two glasses, and they both sat back down at the table. He took a few sips then said, as if it were something he said every day, "I'm going back to New York for awhile."

"Excuse me?" Joy looked at him, her mouth hanging open. She was worried about leaving in the spring and he said this? Joy got up and walked away, turning her back to him. "After what just ... almost just happened and you're leaving?"

He walked over and put his arms around her. She bowed her head and Efram pulled up her hair. Sweat had beaded up on the back of her neck. He kissed her there and let the salty taste linger on his lips, mixing with the sweet taste of the tea. To Joy, the kiss was like a cool breeze.

"It'll only be about two months."

"Two months!" she said, turning to face him. "Efram, that's forever."

"You're so melodramatic!"

"Am I?"

"Yes," he said with a nod and sat back down.

Joy put her hands on her hips and sighed. "Call me old fashioned if you want, but after you profess to love someone and almost make love, you don't add that you're leaving."

"How does me leaving for a couple of months change anything?"

"I don't suppose it does, but ... " Joy held her arms up like she was cupping heavy blankets. "I'll miss you."

"I'll miss you, too. Come here." He pulled Joy to him, and she sat on his lap. Very tenderly, he kissed her and smoothed back her hair. "You're worried that I'm leaving for good. I can see it in your eyes."

"Well ... "

"That's crazy. I meant everything I said to you back at the hotel. I want to be with you, and I don't want to leave, but I have to just for a little while."

"Only two months?"

"Maybe a little less. I don't want to stay in anymore hotels."

"Where will you stay?"

"I still have my apartment."

"When are you leaving?"

"This week, but I promise the time will fly by. You'll have summer session two and then fall classes to keep you busy."

She hugged him tightly. "It will seem like forever."

"But it won't be."

"I love you, Ef."

"I love you, too."

Chapter 14

Marigold

Efram tapped in the security code and the door buzzed, waiting for him to open it. He pushed the door and staggered inside, trying to juggle two suitcases and a pet carrier. The smell of dog fur, paint, and expensive cologne brought back memories. He surveyed the surroundings. His black futon couch beckoned him for a nap. He opened the pet carrier, and Mr. Boogie ran for his fur-lined bed near the window.

"Happy, Boog?" The dog jumped around and danced in circles, chasing his tail. Efram laughed and took a look around. The paintings still hung, lifeless, against the white stucco walls. His easel seemed lonely, the paintbrush on a desk too far away to caress it. As much as it was home, it was also less familiar. When his heels clicked on the floor, it made him think of his place in Wenton. Passing expensive art and neatly organized bookshelves, he went into the kitchen. Spotless, as usual. He opened the barren refrigerator, which released that haven't-been-opened-in-months smell. Mr. Boogie came running in and plopped down beside Efram, wagging his tail.

"Hey, kid, we don't have any food."

Efram retrieved his bags and carried them to the bedroom, passing the spot where *Mine* had reclined against the wall before he moved to Wenton. The bedroom walls were speckled with a few photos of his parents and framed posters of famous paintings that he couldn't get his hands on. He flopped the bags on the bed and sat down, taking a deep breath. He knew what was missing, what would make this place feel more like home – flowers.

※

Marigolds did cheer the place up. He placed them in the kitchen and around the windowsills in the living room. The yellow and orange flowers brightened up the walls and made the paintings sing back to life. Even an old plastic bonsai tree seemed to steal a spark of life from the marigolds and join in the fun.

While he cooked, loving the mixture of scents from the simmering food and the bright flowers on the counter, he would clang the metal spoon against the glass pot and beat out a rhythm that caused Mr. Boogie to run to another room. All the activity made him think of Joy. He imagined her crinkled nose when she bit into something unfamiliar or unappetizing.

The only way he knew how to control his fits of boredom and loneliness was through art. Each night before bed, he waited for sheer, God-sent inspiration, and he sketched Joy. Sometimes in poses that she might find offensive. Other times, he ran to the keyboard in his bedroom; the notes made him cry even if it was just a few taps on the keys. He would run his fingers over the ivory and imagine her skin. He wanted to play her, touch her, and make her sing.

During the day he spent time in the park, letting Mr. Boogie frolic with other dogs, while he fantasized that Joy was strolling with him. At the market, he purchased food that she would have enjoyed. When he stepped out for a movie, he rubbed the arm of the chair, as if in some magical way it could make her feel the softness of his palm.

All he did, every day, was think of her. Every action. Every thought. Joy.

Occasionally, he had a visitor – word had quickly spread that he was in town. He invited a few friends to dinner. Most of them wondered if he was home for good. He explained what had happened to his new home, never mentioning his love for Joy, and that he would return to Wenton to finish his greatest, most personal work ever. They were intrigued, but skeptical.

After only three weeks in the blazing heat of a New York summer, he received news that he had figured would some day arrive. A club buddy spotted Efram buying fruit near his apartment.

"I'm sorry, man," the friend said, patting a puzzled Efram on the back.

"About what?"

The friend put his hand to his mouth. "You don't know? No one told you? I thought you of all people would have known."

"What?" Efram held an orange in his hand and squeezed it. "This is mushy. You call this an orange?" he remarked to the fruit-stand owner.

The owner curled his lip. "Fresh this morning."

"My ass."

"Efram," his friend said and tugged on Efram's shoulder. "Alana died."

Efram turned away from the fruit stand. "What?" He had thought it odd that he had not heard from her. She had always been pushy.

"Overdose. A week ago."

Efram scratched his neck and shook his head. "No. It can't be. She said she was clean."

"Not likely."

"You want oranges? New shipment in back. Just found it," the stand owner said, coming up to them.

"No!" Efram yelled.

"Rotten anyway!" the owner yelled back.

"She visited me in Georgia. Wanted me to do a show," Efram told his friend.

"I heard something about her wanting to do that. She'd had some money problems of late. Look, I'm really sorry, man."

"Yeah, thanks. Hey, I gotta go," Efram patted his friend's back and left. He didn't know how he felt. He wasn't happy, for sure, but he wasn't sad, either. He was a passionate man, but losing Alana left him with as much feeling as losing the rotten orange at the fruit stand.

Efram sat in his room that night, staring at an old photo of Alana. She was standing in front of the sign announcing his first art show. He was so young then, and he thought she was a princess. Now, as he looked at the photograph, he saw the harsh reality. Even then she was withered from too much abuse at her own hands. He remembered punching a guy for saying her skin was as leathery as cowhide. His mother had even said Alana's skin looked like a burnt piece of toast. Now, he could see it too. Efram put the photo back, far back, in his bedroom drawer. Lying down on his bed, he reached over and picked up the snapshot of Joy at the pier. He had caught her expression just before she had fallen into the water. She had such a wide grin, especially for someone complaining about balancing on that post. From his night stand, he took out a sheet of paper and began a letter to Joy.

Chapter 15

Jasmine

"I visited the vet today" was the first line of Efram's first letter to Joy. "Not for me, of course. I don't need shots. Well, maybe, but not for rabies or distemper. Mr. Boogie had his annual check up today, so he's mad at me. He's been ignoring me all day."

Joy smiled to herself. She was so thrilled to receive anything from Efram. She had been unable to concentrate since his departure. It was mid-August and summer session two was in full swing. Algebra was her only subject, but she still had to register for her final classes at the community college.

Joy spent most of her time in bed daydreaming about Efram. She imagined the scene when he would return, and had already picked out a pair of black slacks and a red silk shirt, even if they were too hot to wear on that special day. To curb her longings, and to keep her sanity, she had listened to Smokey Robinson tunes and eaten a lot of cherry cheesecake. Now, she had his words.

The letter continued: "We're getting by just fine. Bored but fine. I decorated the place with lots of plants and flowers. Makes it feel like home."

Joy stopped reading. He had never called Wenton home before.

"There is one essential ingredient that is missing, though. You.

I've settled on the closest I could get. I've been drawing you each night. I enclose one that I think you'll like."

Joy thumbed behind the note and found the sketch. It was a drawing of her as Minnie Mouse. Joy shook her head and laughed.

"I think it is all I can do to curb my loneliness. I'd call, but I'm not sure your Mom likes me too much. I'd ask you to visit, but I know you have school. Still, it is only a little over a month now, and I'm a fairly patient type of guy." Beside this sentence he had drawn a smiley face.

The letter continued with a list of what he'd been doing – reading classics, walking in the park, visiting museums. He inquired about Katie, how she was getting along, and asked Joy to write back. After signing his name with a "Love" that took up the width of the paper, he concluded with a P.S.: "By the way, I found out Alana died of an overdose."

Joy folded the note and leaned back on her bed. She thought it was odd that he closed the letter that way, as if it was an incidental he had to include. She closed her eyes and began composing her letter to him.

CR&O

Efram grabbed Mr. Boogie and headed outside for a stroll in the park, stopping by the mailbox. Sifting through party invitations, bills, and junk mail, he found a letter from Joy. He stuffed it in his back pocket and dumped the rest of the mail in the glove compartment of his rented Honda Accord. Turning on the radio, he headed for Central Park.

Arriving at the park, he stopped for a hot dog and Coke from a street vendor. "Since when did I start eating all this junk food?" he asked Mr. Boogie. Efram found a nice spot and spread a flannel blanket on the ground. The park wasn't very crowded. Only a few people were playing with their pets, or jogging, or making out in the grass. After eating a few pieces of hot dog that Efram gave him, Mr. Boogie trotted away to play with another pug close by.

"Don't worry. He's neutered," Efram shouted to the owner of the female pug. The man smiled and waved. Efram watched Mr. Boogie tumble in the grass with the other dog before he pulled out his letter from Joy.

After taking a long gulp of Coke, he opened the letter. Instantly, he smelled Joy's perfume. Making sure no one was watching, he sniffed the letter. He ran his fingers over the ink and envisioned her sitting at her desk thinking of what to say.

She started the letter, "Tell Mr. Boogie his shots are good for him! Give him a pat on the head for me, Ef."

Efram loved it when she called him "Ef." He could hear her voice as he read the letter.

"I was really surprised to get a letter from you. You can call if you want. My Mom doesn't hate you or anything. She just thinks you'll corrupt me. Ha! Ha!"

Efram smiled. Joy told him about school, how she couldn't concentrate, and how she longed for graduation.

"Fall session starts soon and I'm not in the mood. My mind is elsewhere. Katie is dreading it, too, especially with the baby. Mom's getting a nanny to help out, because she wants Katie to finish high school. Remember the archeological dig? I got another letter from Professor Billings. I have to enroll in this one intro class and I can go on the dig."

When she had mentioned her possible spring plans before he left for New York, Efram had felt a twinge in his heart. He understood why Joy had reacted so intensely to his leaving. He had given her a cliché line about following her dreams, but inside he wanted her with him wherever that might be.

"As for Emily, she got a promotion, so she's doing good. She's not the receptionist anymore. She's moved on to secretary. Naturally, she's thrilled. Mom is getting better. I think she might have a boyfriend. He's a client and calls the house all the time. It takes her mind off Katie and everything. I'm sorry to hear about your friend Alana. I don't know what to say. I hope you are okay. I can't wait until you come back home."

Efram stopped reading and looked up. Mr. Boogie was squirming on his back, enjoying the warm sun. Efram looked at the sky, then back at the trees. He realized his home wasn't New York or Wenton. His home was with Joy. He smiled as he finished reading the letter.

"I can't wait to finish the painting. I mean, after that sketch you sent of me, well, you obviously have loads of talent! See you soon! Love, Joy"

Beside her name she had drawn a heart.

☙❧

Joy stopped by the mall after school to look for a present for Efram. She hated taking cabs, but it was too far to walk. As soon as she stepped into the Disney Store, two voices screamed her name. Carrying large bags from Everything's a Dollar, two high school classmates, Lea McDonald and Winnie Draper, approached her. Both had been cheerleaders in school, but now Winnie worked at a travel agency as a file clerk and Lea sold cosmetics at a department store.

"Hi. Haven't seen y'all in a while," Joy said, impatiently tapping her foot.

Winnie droned on about getting free travel, while Lea bitched about snooty women who expected her to work miracles.

"You know, these old hags think make-up can change the tides or something." Lea's own make-up was as thick as molasses, clumped and sticky, especially around the many pimples on her forehead. Joy grimaced. "So, Joy, what've ya been up to?" Lea asked, pulling on her red hoop earrings.

"Oh, nothing much. I'm working on a degree in archeology."

"I remember that. You always liked playing in the dirt," Winnie said and laughed.

"Well, it's not the travel industry, I suppose," Joy responded. "Look, I have some shopping to do. See you later." She waved to them and went inside the store. They shrugged their shoulders and walked away. Joy twisted her belt loop and frowned. She wished she had thought of something clever to say. Efram would have taken them down, she thought. He always knew what to say. She took a deep breath and turned her attention to choosing his gift.

The store was filled with everything a child would adore, which she knew would suit Efram just fine. *It's a Small World* skipped along on the store's sound system. Joy bopped her head to it while she dug through a pile of stuffed toys from Mickey Mouse to Flounder in

The Little Mermaid. Nothing seemed right. There were key chains, coffee mugs, and buttons, but none matched Efram's personality. Then, on a shelf she'd have to stand on her toes to reach, there was the perfect gift. A Goofy hat. It had large floppy ears hanging off the sides and a big tongue hanging in the front. After purchasing it, she bought a card on the way home and inscribed it "A Goofy hat for a goofy person." The gift would be perfect revenge for drawing her as Minnie Mouse.

When she got home, the mail was late. It was Efram's turn to write, but she wanted to send the hat right away. She threw her book bag on her bedroom floor and pulled Efram's hat out of the sack. She put it on her head and looked in the mirror. "Maybe I'll keep it for me," she said to herself. The neighbor's dog barked, and Joy knew that the mailman was heading for her house. She put the hat away and went outside.

Playing it cool, pretending to arrange a plant, Joy waited until the mailman was out of sight before she ran to the box. Bills, a Sears ad, and a package from Efram.

Before she made it back indoors, Joy started opening the package. She ran to her room and closed the door. Falling on her stomach on the bed, she tore the box open. Securely surrounded in bubble wrap, a black bottle fell out. She ripped away the wrapping to find it was a bottle of perfume. "Joy" was hand-painted in red script along with a drawing of a white flower. Opening the top, she squirted the perfume on her wrist. Jasmine. Joy put the perfume on her night stand and read the letter.

"Dear Joy (such a fitting name)," the note began.

"Did you know that Cleopatra soaked her ship's sails in jasmine to seduce Marc Antony? I bet you did, archeology girl. When I think of archeologists I always think Egypt, so I thought this scent was fitting for you. You always smell so nice, and I often think you smell like honeysuckle. Don't ask me why. Anyway, I have a friend who designs perfumes, so I had him whip this up for you. I hope you like it. It was specially made just for you. Tré snooty! Of course, now I owe this guy a major favor for concocting this for me on the spur of the moment! Ha! Ha! Like he'll ever see it."

Joy took the perfume in her hands again and squirted it all around her. The fragrance hung in the air, and Joy reclined in her bed for a moment. She knew jasmine was a known aphrodisiac and knew the

Cleopatra story. Efram held a power over her that did not require extra stimulation. She fanned out the sheets on her bed and let the covers mix with the hovering scent. Fully conquered, she curled up and read the rest of his letter.

It continued: "Miss me? Mr. Boogie says hi. I think the cement sidewalks and fire hydrants are starting to get boring for him. He prefers a good tree any day. We went to the park today and I made a discovery. While Boog was entertaining another pug (ahem), I ate a hot dog (not even a soy weenie!) and read your letter. I was looking for something when I left New York, and I thought I could get that in Wenton. I wanted to find inspiration. I wanted to find peace. I wanted proof that the world isn't crazy. I found that in you."

A lump welled up in her throat.

"You make me feel like a kid with a snow cone in one hand and a new baseball card in the other. I have it all. You're so wonderful. I lie in bed every night and can't stop fantasizing about you. Being with you. Kissing you. Loving you. Each night I sketch you. I imagine you in different places. Or the two of us together. When I draw you, I feel you. I know that you know this. When we work on the painting, I can tell just by the way you fidget that you are aware of what I'm painting and thinking. Remember the day before I left? That night we danced on the porch to that Aaron Neville song after the workmen left? The mosquitoes were so bad and I had to make a mad dash to the drugstore for bug repellent. Did you know that the whole time I was thinking about how beautiful your legs were even with the little red bites all over them? I will continue to desire you. I wish I could make love to you through my letters, but I'll wait, instead, until we are together working on the portrait. I long to see your handwriting again, which flows like you – smooth, feminine, and pretty. Love, Efram"

Joy folded the letter. Now her present for him seemed silly.

Chapter 16

Rose

J oy stood on her porch like Aphrodite surveying her kingdom. Rose petals fell to the ground as she plucked them from the bush that nearly slithered up the porch beam. The plant had been there since she was a child. As vibrant as it was, it seemed almost languid now, as if waiting for a drink. It was so hot that Joy thought the wings of the bugs fluttering around her head might melt. The heat aggravated her, but she had been annoyed since the night before. The autumn term was underway. Homework piled up on her desk. The paperwork had arrived to enroll for the spring. She had tossed and turned in bed so much that her sheets looked like a cotton tornado. Like an amateur actor anxiously awaiting her first cue, Joy had huddled in bed, thinking about the next step in her life. Efram was expected back in two days.

    The sky shot forth rays of sunshine from what seemed to be the devil's pit. Sitting on the steps, Joy twisted a strand of her hair and pulled it into her mouth. Even though the sweat made her lips purse, she continued to roll the hair on her tongue. More of the salty liquid dripped into her mouth as it rolled from her upper lip. Arching her back, she got up to go inside. The air conditioner would relieve her like an army sergeant being pulled off war duty. Before going in, Joy picked up the rose petals that she had let fall to the ground. They were so soft and gentle, just a slight pull and they would tear. A small pink petal split soundlessly in two as Joy pulled it apart. Releasing its fragrance, it turned red at the tear as if it were bleeding. She stared at the two pieces resting in her palm for only a brief moment before she put them, one by one, into her mouth. The heavy aroma radiated in her mouth like an atom bomb. Careful not to touch the petals with her teeth, she let them lie on her tongue until they had almost melted. Then she swallowed them. Holding the other petals in her hand, she clutched them tightly before putting them in the pockets of her faded blue jeans. Opening the screen door, she gave a final look at the deep blue sky that was not like a serene crystal lake but like dry ice, scalding and lingering.

Inside, she flopped down on the sofa only to be disturbed by the telephone. "Who the hell could it be?" she muttered as she got up to answer it. "Yeah?" she said into the receiver. The voice on the other end was quiet for a moment. Joy sighed and put her hand on her hip. "Hello," she said to the silence.

"Joy?"

Again, silence.

"Efram? Is that you?"

"Hey, guess where I am?"

Joy hesitated and clenched her fists. "I'll be there in a minute."

She was surprised that Efram had arrived early, but she was as pleased as a lottery winner. The sun winked at her and reflected off the puddles she encountered as she took the back trail to Efram's house. She ran so fast even the swiftest gazelle would have felt itself surpassed. Her heart pounded, her muscles were taut, and the sweat continued to roll down her body and make her look exhausted. But she wasn't exhausted. She was excited, as excited as she'd ever been in her life. As she pushed away the heavy green bushes and vines, his house came into view. There it stood as always, magnificent and regal, embodying everything that she and Efram had become. The fresh paint job made it almost glow white.

Efram came out onto the porch wearing an angel's smile, wide and gleaming. He reclined his elbows on the railing and waited for Joy to conclude her stampede across the yard. He tossed aside the stem he'd been playing with as Joy bombarded up the steps.

"No one's ever gonna nickname you tortoise with a sprint like that," he said, giving Joy a hearty embrace.

"I ran all the way over," she said, gasping for breath.

"I missed you, too," Efram said, running his fingertips deep into her back, so deep that Joy thought he could feel the crevices of her spine. Passionately, Joy kissed him. Efram raised her feet from the ground and tried to bring her as close to his body as possible. Their hearts, like their bodies sticky from the heat, fought for stability.

Efram slowly, very slowly, released her bottom lip from his mouth. Joy bowed her head, then placed her ear against his chest. "I can feel your heart, Efram."

"Me, too." Tenderly, he stroked her back. "You're wearing the perfume."

"Yes! I love it!"

"It smells good on you."

Efram led her indoors where his art supplies were in their proper place, and the window seat was bare without its centerpiece. Roses were strewn all over the floor.

"In the mood?" Efram asked, walking over to his easel. Joy smiled and went to the bathroom to change and wash the sweat from her hair.

In the bathroom, the new furnishings caught her off guard. The room was slightly bigger than before. A rubber tree plant was in the corner. The antique claw foot tub was still there but outfitted with shiny pristine fixtures. An avant-garde shower was installed opposite. Joy thought it looked like an upright, glass-covered coffin.

"Efram, I love the new sink!" she yelled. To Joy, it looked like something that would be in a fancy hotel with chrome fixtures and a marble top. No doubt it cost him a fortune, Joy thought.

"Thanks!" he yelled back.

When she emerged, Efram realized that his memory had done her an injustice. Joy was even more beautiful than when he'd left her. She took her rightful spot on the window seat and struck the pose that had now become a part of her. She noticed there were small stains on the floor all around her.

"What are those stains?" she asked.

"From the water and the flowers on the floor after the storm," Efram answered, adjusting his supplies.

"Why didn't you tell them to refinish it?"

Efram grinned. "I like them there. Doesn't this room smell like flowers?"

Joy nodded as Efram approached the window seat to adjust her outfit. With one hand he positioned her collar, with the other he juggled his palette. Efram had told her that his palette was specially made for him, since he often worked with common house paint. It was designed to hold the paint in small indented areas to keep it from sliding off or drying up. A bead of sweat glided down her neck to her chest, and then hid underneath the sheer white cloth. Efram watched it while he arranged her dress. His fingers stroked the material, then his hand, like a lone being, took control of his emotions. He caressed Joy's neck, then cupped her right breast tenderly, barely touching it. Realizing what he'd done, he jerked his hand away and dropped the palette onto her lap. She gasped as the paint was quickly absorbed into the flimsy material and stuck to her skin. The green, the blue, and the yellow formed thick splashes of color on her dress, while the red streamed down her leg, mixing with her sweat and staining the pillow of the window seat. Joy rubbed one finger in the red paint and was about to smear it on Efram's face when he grabbed her wrist. Taking her other wrist as well, he raised her from the window seat and then let her arms fall over his shoulders. She locked her arms in place and wrapped one leg securely around his. Only the ceiling fan and the curtains trapped in the breeze made a noise as they kissed.

In his bedroom, Efram removed her dress. The thin material fell away like petals falling from a white rose and landed quietly on the floor. Joy tried to cover herself; Efram stopped her, then stepped back to admire her. Joy blushed and bit her lip as Efram walked around her, as if studying a piece of art. He noticed the length of her legs, the curve of her knees, and each little toe. With his eyes, he caressed her, and Joy shivered. She closed her eyes as Efram moved closer, wanting to touch her, but he wouldn't allow himself the pleasure until he imagined the taste and feel of each part of her, particularly her belly button, which he found to be like the tiny opening of a bud. His eyes lingered until they fell, casually, upon her breasts. He had seen them peep through her dress since the painting began, spending many nights imagining them totally uncovered. He turned her around. With her back to him, Joy bowed her head, and

Efram let his fingers gently run down her spine like a keyboard. This time Joy forgot any left-over inhibitions and raised her head; he leaned around and kissed her cheek, cupping one breast and pinching its nipple. Joy moaned. Efram's eyes, never failing on their mission, took in the curve of her back, the crease in her bottom, and, once again, her legs.

He stepped back; the tips of his fingers resided on her hips. "Joy, turn around," he commanded, his voice cracking. Joy complied. She moved closer to him and rested her head on his chest. Efram rubbed her head, tenderly at first, but the strokes grew rougher and deeper as he continued. He put his arms around her waist and squeezed her tightly.

"Let me make love to you like the moon, slowly rising, makes love to the sky. Like the wind caresses the trees. Like the waves fuck the ocean," Efram said, holding her so close she thought she would crack. Joy closed her eyes; Efram carried her to the bed.

Joy let out a little whimper as Efram climbed on top of her. He straddled her and gave her a fierce look, then placed both hands on her face and kissed her hard. Throwing her arms around his neck, she held him close. It seemed impossible to her to feel this close to anyone. After kissing her entire face, Efram snuggled into her neck. Joy moaned as Efram kissed harder. Sitting back up, he stared into her eyes. He ran his fingers down her face and tapped her nose. She smiled as he let his hands glide down to her breasts, which he took, one in each hand, and squeezed gently.

"Efram," Joy sighed.

Running his hands over her face and into her hair, Efram bent down to kiss her nipples, letting the tip of his tongue savor them. Joy bucked underneath him and he responded with more amorous kisses. The salty sweat had mixed with her perfume, making him want to devour her even more. Her toes curled at each nibble he took. He worked his way down her stomach before rolling her over. Joy giggled.

"What's so funny?" Efram asked her, burying his head next to hers. She didn't respond. "This?" he asked and slapped her bottom.

Joy jumped up and reclined on her side. "Hey! Do I look like a masochist?"

Efram ignored her remark and admired the way her belly button looked smushed by her weight. "I have an outy," he said.

"What?"

"My belly button protrudes out," he said and raised his shirt.

Joy grinned and tugged on the button of his pants. Efram raised his eyebrows as Joy followed the little sprigs of hair that led underneath his pants. She undid the snap, then he caught her hand. One by one, he sucked each of her fingers like he was enjoying a popsicle. Joy moved closer.

"Be gentle with me. I'm shy," he muttered with a laugh.

"Right," Joy murmured. Efram nuzzled into her neck again. Her voice shook as she said, "Ef?"

He mumbled a response.

"I'm, um ... " she muttered, her voice cracking. She felt as she had when she saw Efram for the first time, just a few feet away, buying watercolors at Brooke's. "I've never, you know ... this is my first time." Her voice continued to break, trailing off.

Efram grinned. "No? You're kidding!"

Joy lifted her head. "Efram ... "

"Come on." He continued to grin, brushing her hair with his fingers. "It shows."

Lightly, Joy slapped him on the chest. "Hush."

He raised himself on one arm. "Nervous?"

Joy shrugged. "Not with you."

He smiled. "So the whips and cattle prod won't bother you?"

"Lose the whips. Keep the prod."

"I like you, girl."

"I like you more."

"Sly devil." Efram kissed her. It felt like warm rain falling into Joy as if she were the ocean. It lingered on her lips for an instant before it merged with her. Then, with a wave of pounding kisses, they made love, not stopping for the sunlight that faded as it moved across the floor.

Chapter 17

Briar

Efram had picked the wrong day to drive to Atlanta. The famed art collector Evan C. Isamorone was in the museum. Efram hated him. Isamorone, greedy and shallow, was yet another example of the world of art that Efram despised. The museum itself was not. Efram loved great art, loved to look at it, and appreciated the work of others.

An eclectic mix – Jackson Pollock, Georgia O'Keeffe, and even Efram Corbet – was part of Isamorone's collection on display for October, but it wasn't his own work that Efram wanted Joy to see. He wanted to show her more of his world. He had needed to get her out of her environment as well. The Baxter house was as infected with tension as the C.D.C with germs. Katie's demands drove everyone crazy. Beverly bickered constantly. Even the ever-calm Emily had threatened to elope to escape. Joy moped around Efram's house, complaining about what was going on at home, so that it was difficult to put finishing touches on the painting. Most of the time, when Joy threw him a harsh look, he felt it was directed at him alone.

"Efram, why don't you ever buy anything good anymore? There's never any junk food around," she had grumbled to him one day after school.

"What are you? My wife?" he had growled back. He was joking, but Joy didn't find it funny and walked off.

There was nothing, he thought, that he could do to make her feel better, so he arranged a getaway. The museum, a favorite place of escape for him, was one of the best ways he knew.

The paintings hung naked to the eyes of strangers. Efram and Joy strolled the halls, careful not to step on college students who sat on the floor sipping coffee and taking notes. Efram stopped and explained each painting as they passed it. Some of the work Joy loved, some Efram loved, and some they both hated. Efram went into a tirade about one artist he particularly hated, saying he'd slept his way to the top.

It didn't take Isamorone, a middle-aged man with an affinity for red leather jackets, long to spot Efram. He hurried towards them, saluting as he ran. Efram muttered "Shit" just before he was engaged in a firm handshake. Isamorone then hugged Efram and gave him a hard pat on the back.

Putting on his fake charm, Efram said, "Hi, Evan."

Isamorone pulled down his John Lennon style glasses and looked at Joy. "Madam," he said and took her hand. "Corbet, who is this lovely creature?" He pronounced Efram's last name as if it were French, with a silent T.

Efram ran a finger down Joy's cheek. "This is my friend Joy," he answered. "She's my new neighbor."

With her shoulder, Joy rubbed her cheek and felt queasy. She curled her upper lip, attempting to smile.

"Such a wonderful name. And neighbors! How quaint!" Sipping champagne, he looked at Efram. "I heard that you'd moved. I didn't know it was Atlanta. We should have dinner. I'll be in town a few more days after the show closes next week," Isamorone said, patting Efram's shoulder.

"I don't live in Atlanta. I'm just visiting," Efram replied.

"So, how's your new life? Picket fence yet?"

"Only in my paintings. Which," Efram added, "I'm sure you'll buy."

"Efram, is that sarcasm I detect?" Isamorone responded. "I have one of your paintings here, you know. You aren't planning to take it down and carry it out, are you?"

"Funny, Evan. Real funny."

Joy tugged on Efram's shirt. "Ef, can we look at that painting over there?"

Efram smiled. "Sure. Nice to see you, Evan. We're going to have a look around."

Isamorone waved goodbye, and Efram headed towards the painting he thought Joy wanted to see. "That one?" he asked.

"I just wanna see your painting. I made that up, so we could leave."

Efram gasped. "Girl, you mean you lied? I love you." He kissed her; Joy pulled back. "What's the matter?"

"Nothing," she said and shrugged. All she could think about was his answer to her question during the drive up.

"You've gotta go for your dreams, Joy," he had told her, while sucking down a bag of cashews. "You've wanted to do this forever. You can't hold back."

"Yeah, I guess I should," she had answered, wishing he would say, "No, stay. Be with me!" Instead, Efram was as matter-of-fact in his belief that Joy should go to Texas as her mother was in her belief that Joy should not. She had spent the rest of the drive staring at the small calendar that hung from the visor. The date was October 20 and it sat in her mind like a blocked artery. She leaned her head on the window; it bobbed with the bumps on the road. She hoped the jarring would jerk her body back into childhood. The tears had stopped in her eyes days ago, waiting for her orders to flow. She still refused to command them, nor would she command her voice to speak now. She had ignored Efram's chatter about the presidential election and stared at the fertile farmland before her. Large stalks of corn, black-and-white spotted cows, and clean white barns with fresh bales of hay went past them as they drove, but there was always another farm to quickly replace the memory of the last. All Joy wanted to see was a barren field – nothing impregnated with life.

"It's not my favorite, and I'm not sure you want to see it, but I'll show it to you," Efram said, jolting her out of her thoughts and back to the museum. He put his hands in his pockets and motioned with his head for Joy to follow him.

When they reached a painting of a naked middle-aged woman with bleached-blond hair, they stopped. The woman in the portrait leaned against a pillar in an art gallery, as if she was trying desperately to be a classic beauty. However, the rigidness of her body, the steely look in her eyes, and the bulging veins on her feet made her fall terribly short of being Venus in a Botticelli painting.

"This is Alana," Efram said quietly, looking around the room.

"Oh." Joy leaned in closer to observe the painting.

"Alana loved it. She was too blind to see the reality of it. Like metal, she is cold."

Joy glanced at the name of the painting: *Alana Lisa*. "That's her last name? Lisa?"

Efram slapped his leg hard and laughed. "Hell no! Think about it. *She* named it. Shows how arrogant she really was!" Joy looked confused and shrugged her shoulders. "Joy ... most famous painting on earth?"

"Oh, *Mona Lisa*!" Joy shook her head. "How vain!"

"Weird to think she's dead."

"You wanna look at something else?" Thinking about Alana and her own painting with Efram, she wondered how many of his models he fell in love with.

Efram put his arm around her. "You want to go for lunch? I know a great veggie place."

"Whatever."

When they got in the car, Efram turned on the heater. The autumn air was chilly, and Efram shivered when the heat hit his face. "You said veggie was okay? There's a place called The Colbert Diner. Really good. Home-style and exotic vegetarian dishes. I've been there before. Really nice people who own it. Jack and Christie. I think they were going to open an old-time juke joint next door, but I'm not ... "

Joy interrupted him. "On average, how many of your models in your paintings have you slept with?"

"Whoa, Joy! Where did that come from?" He pushed back his seat, undid his seat belt, and turned to face her.

"I'm waiting." Joy rubbed her palms against her jeans. "You sleep with me."

"You know that's different."

Joy raised her eyebrows. "Is it?"

"Look, Joy. Most of my models wanted to be in *Vogue* or *Cosmopolitan* and saw me as a stepping stone. They'd come in, push out their bust, and pout. It annoyed me. I never slept with my models." Then, feeling guilty, he added, "Well, okay, some. I slept with some, but that was then."

"Then? It's going on with me right now!"

"Don't get jealous on me. What brought this on? Alana? Dammit! I knew I shouldn't have shown you that."

"It has nothing to do with that. Just forget about it."

Efram huffed and started up the car.

Again, on the way to the restaurant, she studied the calendar, turning the pages forward, then back. Her application paperwork was due the first week of November, so she had to send it in immediately. She looked at the date for a moment and continued to flip the pages. When she turned back to June, Efram's attention shifted from the road to the calendar. June 10 was circled – the day he first drove into Wenton. Joy flipped the pages quickly, like she was making a cartoon of the days as they flew by.

As Joy held open the calendar for January, the car swerved off the road. Hitting a flimsy fence, it plowed into a cotton field covered in vines.

"Joy, you okay?" Efram reached over and rubbed her arm. She held the calendar, yanked loose by the impact, in her hand. "I'm sorry. I wasn't paying attention."

"You okay?" she asked back.

He smiled, patted her leg, then said, "I'm going to survey the damage." He got out of the car; Joy followed him, only to get pricked by briar bushes.

"Ah! Ouch, Efram! I'm stuck!"

Efram climbed over the car hood and jumped down in front of her. He pulled the weeds away from her legs, then sat her on the hood and removed burrs from her socks.

"See." He pulled the socks down. "Not a scratch. No blood."

"Efram," she said, her tears ignoring her orders.

"It's okay." His voice was soft like a fingertip. He kissed her cheek. "Everything will be fine."

She mumbled and wiped her eyes.

Efram opened the door, reached into the glove compartment, and pulled out a tissue, knocking out a map as well. Before he handed Joy the tissue, he stared at the map. It was still open to Georgia. The edges were crinkled and worn. He held out the tissue to Joy. While she dried her eyes, he flipped through the map, slowly, until he found Texas. He left it open, leaned over the seats, and put it in the driver's side door pocket.

"Hey, Joy, there's some honeysuckle. What do you say we eat a few before we get this back on the road?"

Joy nodded. Efram picked her up and carried her to safety.

Chapter 18

Bridal Wreath

The blood flowed out of her body like a healing spring, dammed for years but now unleashed. As she sat on the toilet, her elbows on her knees, she leaned over and rested her head in her hands. She sighed and said to God, "Thank you."

"Let me in!" Katie yelled, banging on the door. Her voice was frantic.

"Geez! Hang on a sec," Joy yelled back, getting herself together.

"Now!"

Joy buttoned her pants and opened the door. "Oh, come on! No one has to go that damn bad!"

Katie, tears smearing her makeup, clutched her stomach. "I think it's labor!"

Joy grabbed her sister by the shoulders. "Are you sure?"

Katie fell into her arms. "Call Mom!"

Joy helped her to lean against the sink. "It can't be time yet."

"You gonna argue about this or get help?" Katie slumped down.

Joy left the bathroom and dialed her mother's number. She chewed on her lip as if it were a pacifier. Katie had closed the bathroom door, but Joy could hear her crying.

"Come on, pick up," Joy said into the receiver until a cheery voice on the other end answered. "Beverly Baxter, please. It's an emergency!" Joy said, tapping her foot and pulling on her lip.

"I'm sorry, she's showing a house," the woman said, completely calm.

"Shit! It's an emergency. I'll use her beeper." Joy slammed the phone down. "Idiots!" She scanned the numbers taped to the wall above the phone, then quickly picked up the phone again and punched in the number. Before it started to ring, Katie screamed. Dropping the phone, Joy opened the bathroom door. Katie sat on the edge of the toilet, blood running down her legs. With the palm of her hand, Katie pushed at the blood as if it were lava. It smeared all over her legs.

"Joy, what's happening?"

"I don't know. Everything will be fine. I promise."

Joy picked up the phone and dialed 911.

☙❧

Efram was painting the stains on his floor from the roses when Joy called. The phone startled him, but he did not smudge the painting. Looking lovingly at the red paint on his hands, he put down the brush, then answered the phone.

"Yes?"

"Efram! I'm at the hospital. Katie's miscarried or something. I don't understand."

"You want me to come down?"

"Please. Mom and Emily aren't here."

"I'll be there."

Efram arrived at the hospital thirty minutes later. He stopped in the hospital gift shop and bought the family a bouquet of tulips. For Joy, he bought a Snickers, a Dr Pepper, and a stuffed bear that held a heart.

He found Joy in the ER waiting room, sitting alone with her hands in her lap on the worn blue faux-leather couch. Across from her, two toddlers pulled on the lap of an old woman wearing a rhinestone-studded jacket. The woman tickled the boys and they squealed, running past Joy, who ignored them, to a knocked-over cardboard box surrounded by old toys, many of them dirty or broken. In the corner, a man stopped reading a magazine and started to get up when he saw Efram come in, then he sighed and resumed reading.

"Joy." Efram walked towards her. She straightened up and smiled. Sitting down beside her, he stroked her head. "How is she?"

"They're inducing labor. An incompetent or incomplete cervix or something like that caused it." Her lip quivered. "It's going to be ... stillborn."

Efram put the gifts on the coffee table in front of them and put his arm around her. "It'll be all right, Joy."

"I feel so bad for Katie, but I don't think she was ready for this responsibility. None of us were." Joy looked at Efram and tugged on the hem of her shirt. "Is it bad to feel this way? Does it sound cruel? I believe things happen for a reason."

"It's okay, Joy. You don't have to feel guilty."

"I know. I feel so sad to lose the baby, but at the same time I think it wasn't meant to be."

"Some things are not. Some things are." He pulled her close and rubbed her back. She nuzzled against him.

"Is your mom here yet?"

"She's showing a house. I left a message at the office and on her beeper. She's probably on her way. I can't find Emily. They said she took the day off. I called Jonathan's house, but she wasn't there either."

The children screamed and started throwing a ball around the waiting room. Efram smiled at them. "Shhhh," he whispered. They laughed and ran to him, handing him the ball. They jumped up and down as he held it in the air. Across the room, their grandmother apologized and tried to get the kids to return to her. They wouldn't budge and tried to climb in Efram's lap. Joy sat back and watched him. He giggled and stuck out his tongue, causing the kids to squeal. It made some sense to Joy that Efram would be good with kids. She had seen him react to Mr. Boogie with the same playful affection. Still, he was so particular; Joy couldn't imagine Efram with a house full of kids running around, knocking over paint cans and rearranging his kitchen utensils. Joy giggled at the thought.

"How old are they?" Efram asked their grandmother. He patted the children's heads, then rolled the ball across the floor.

"Little Michael just turned two. A joker, he is. Howard is three.

So much beautiful curly hair, that one." The woman clasped her hands together as the children ran back to her. Opening her mouth wide, she raised her eyebrows and took the ball from them.

"Cute," Efram said.

"Getting a new baby sister today," the woman said, her eyes widening. "Mother's in labor since four this morning. I brought the kids up to the hospital an hour ago. Poor father is in Kentucky, trying to get a flight out." She rubbed Michael's head. "Ready to meet your new sister?"

"You like kids, Ef?" Joy asked, eyeing the stuffed bear on the table.

Efram picked up the bear and handed it to her. "For you. And yes, I like kids. Does that surprise you?" The boys ran back to Efram, holding up the ball. He took it and tossed it across the room.

"Sort of." Joy reached for the candy and soda. "This for me, too?"

Efram nodded. "I knew you'd be hungry. You're always hungry."

With a crack in her voice, she said, "Ef, I'm glad you're here." She leaned against his shoulder and he wrapped his arm around her. "I thought I was gonna end up like her, too." She bit her lip.

"Like who?"

"Katie. You know, pregnant. And that you'd be mad, but I just got my period today, so it's okay," Joy whispered. "It's a couple weeks late and I was worried."

Efram was quiet for a moment. Joy opened the soda and took a drink, trying to ignore his silence.

"Why didn't you talk to me?" he asked her softly, so the others in the room couldn't hear. The children had quieted after finding a Barbie to dress up.

Joy shrugged. "I was worried how you'd feel."

"How did you think I'd feel?"

Joy put down the soda. "That you'd leave me."

"Let's go out in the hall." He took her hand and led her into the brightly lit, but cold and silent, hallway. He found a red couch that looked more like an overgrown foot rest, and they sat down. Leaning close to

Joy, he said, "You should have told me. Why were you worried anyway? We use protection."

"That doesn't always work."

"You were probably late because of all the stuff that's going on in your life. That happens. You've been under a lot of stress."

"Joy! How is Katie?" Beverly's heels clicked loudly on the cement floor as she ran towards them. Her handbag flopped up and down on her back, nearly hitting an RN walking by with a tray full of IV bags. "Is she all right?" Beverly asked as her daughter approached her. "What room?" She looked at Efram as if she was scanning him for weapons.

"They're inducing labor. I'm still waiting to hear something."

"Dear god."

"Mom, the baby ... will be stillborn."

Beverly frowned and sighed. She bit her lip hard, trying to stifle the tears.

"Why don't I get some coffee," Efram said and patted Joy on the back. "I'll leave you two alone."

When Efram was out of earshot, she looked at Joy and remarked, "What's he doing here? He's not family." The tears were harder to control.

"I called him. I was alone." Joy sat beside her and held her mother's hand as she wept. The last time Joy remembered her mother crying was at her father's funeral. Seeing a parent cry is always surreal and it made Joy uneasy. "Let's go back into the waiting room." Beverly dried her eyes, and Joy pushed open the door to the waiting room and they went inside.

Beverly sat down and slung her purse on the coffee table, barely missing Joy's Dr Pepper.

Joy opened her candy bar. "I can't find Emily."

"What do you mean you can't find her?"

"They said she took the day off."

Beverly scratched her head. "Odd."

Cradling two cups of coffee, Efram opened the swinging door with his backside. "I'll just put these here," he said, putting the coffee on the table. He smiled at Beverly. "I'm sorry about what happened to Katie. Let me know if you need anything." He nodded and left the room.

"Ef, wait!" Joy picked up her stuffed toy and pointed at the flowers. "Mom, Ef brought you those." Beverly cradled the flowers and stared at them blankly.

Joy found Efram in the hallway reading a bulletin board covered with tips on lowering cholesterol, information on preventing STDs, and an odd message in red, scribbled on yellowed construction paper: "Look to the belly." She tapped Efram on the shoulder, startling him.

"How is your mom?"

"Weepy."

"Considering the circumstances, you have to give her this one. She's upset." Efram put his arm around her.

"Miss Baxter?" a voice called. Joy turned around. Two doctors approached her. The one who had admitted Katie, Dr. DeLana, said, "Ma'am, you can see your sister now. She's fine." She checked her clipboard. "Room 303."

Joy sighed and glanced at the ceiling. "Thanks." Motioning towards the waiting room, she said, "My mom is here. Don't you want to talk to her?"

"Yes, shall we?" The doctor led them back into the waiting room where Beverly sat looking at photos in her wallet. She put the wallet back in her purse and stood up to greet them.

"Is she okay?"

"Fine. She'll need to stay overnight, and we'd like to continue to see her for a while. I'm sorry to have to inform you that the baby was stillborn."

Beverly nodded.

She introduced the student doctor with her: "This is Sarah Johnson. She's doing a psychiatry rotation. Great with teens. She'd love to work with Katie and your family."

"Ma'am," Dr. Johnson said.

Beverly shook her hand. "I just want to see Katie now."

Katie was asleep when they entered the room, but the sound of her mother's heels woke her. Her eyes were heavy and dark like she'd been in a fight. She raised herself on her elbows and moaned. Efram grimaced, clasped his hands together in front of him, and looked around the room. The starch white paint on the walls was clean and new.

Medical machines beeped and flickered. A curtain went around part of the room to separate an empty bed. He looked for a seat, but the only one available was filled with towels and bed sheets, so he rocked back and forth on his feet while Beverly and Joy approached Katie.

"Honey, how do you feel?"

"My baby is gone," she whispered.

"Just rest."

☙❧

Efram drove Joy home at Beverly's request. The ride back was quiet. He stopped at McDonald's and bought Joy a Quarter Pounder combo and a chicken salad for himself. Joy ate most of the fries on the way home. When they arrived, she checked the mail and found a letter from Professor Billings. Once inside, she dropped the bag of food on the table, and Efram sat down while she ripped open the letter. The fee for the archeological dig was being raised by one hundred dollars. She folded the letter and told Efram.

"That okay?" he asked, taking out his salad.

"Yeah. You want a drink?"

"Just water, thanks."

As they ate, Joy kept watching Efram. He ate his salad, not digging around in it as if searching for something, but going straight for the right piece, the perfect piece, that fit on his fork. Joy dumped the last two fries on the wax paper from her hamburger. Lining them up, she chose the one she wanted. The other, which had a burnt spot on the end, she put back in the box and threw in the trash.

"The painting will be done soon," she said.

"It's my best work. I love our painting. I want to take it to New York. Not sell it, of course, because it's too personal." He looked at her. To Joy, he always seemed to stare into her. "I want to do a show next year. Show off some pieces I've been hiding. Show our painting, too."

"Will you visit me in Texas?"

"I could do better than that."

"What do you mean?"

"I could come with you."

"To Texas?"

"Seriously, Joy, I don't want to leave you either. I've been thinking about it a lot. The painting will be done soon, but we won't. We have to face it now. What to do."

"I'd love for you to come with me."

"I know it's a big step. You can think about it if you want." He held up his glass as if he were toasting the decision.

The cat-shaped clock on the wall ticked slowly and Joy smiled.

∞

Joy felt her mother's breath as Beverly leaned over to kiss her.

"Mom?" Joy said, coming out of a deep sleep, and smelling coffee brewing. For a second, she felt around the bed for Efram, realizing he had gone home in the night. Making love to him in her own room had been intoxicating and liberating, but seeing her mother sitting on the edge of her bed made her embarrassed.

"Hey, sleepy," Beverly said and rubbed her daughter's shoulder.

Joy sat up and scratched her neck. All night she had dreamed of adventures with Efram. A particularly profound one featured Efram taking her hand and pointing to a road. The passage was covered with flowers – it looked similar to the trails behind her house – and a large arrow with "Now" written across it. As they walked, the road transformed into a highway and they flew above it. She did not see any specific place ahead of them. Instead, she saw the entire world, as if she and Efram were floating high above the earth.

"I found Emily," Beverly said, knocking Joy out of her memory. "You're not going to believe what she did."

Joy stared at her mother, waiting for an answer, but instinctively she already knew.

"They eloped. I got hold of Jon's mother soon after you left. They're in Vegas! Sneaky! I spoke to Emily, told her not to leave her honeymoon."

"She's been threatening it for a long time." Joy rubbed her groggy eyes and yawned.

"More like dropping hints!"

"And Katie?"

"I'm going back to get her later. The doctor wants to check her once more before she leaves." Beverly looked around the room. "I brought doughnuts, if you want some."

Joy got out of bed and followed her mother out of the room. She shivered at the cold air as Beverly opened the door to put out a saucer of milk for a stray cat that had recently made the Baxter home its own. Huddling up in the kitchen chair, her legs drawn up against her, Joy took a doughnut.

Beverly took a deep breath of morning air and remarked, "Lovely day out." After pouring a cup of coffee, she took a seat opposite Joy and said, "Tell Efram I said thank you for the flowers."

Joy raised an eyebrow. "I will."

"It was nice of him to ... "

"Why don't you like him?"

Beverly took a sip of coffee and answered, "I never said I didn't." Her hair was pulled back loosely with two bobby pins on either side; she kept pushing her hair over her ears. With her clothes wrinkled and disheveled, Joy had never seen her mother so unkempt. Like a television star, she woke up flawless.

"I just said he's too worldly for you." Beverly sighed.

"You don't want *me* to be worldly."

Her mother smiled, a smile that completely changed her appearance from tired mother to pageant queen. "You like Efram a lot?"

"I love him, Mom."

Her mother shrugged and got up to put away the dishes that had been drying on a towel since the day before.

Joy frowned and shook her head. "He's coming with me to Texas."

"I see." She nodded. "That's a big step. You're only twenty. Living with a man ... "

"You said you didn't want me out there alone. Besides I'll be twenty-one soon."

"I still think you're getting into something you're not ready for, but you're old enough to make your own decisions, even if I don't agree."

"It's my decision to make, mistake or not. That's what life's about."

"I just want you to be happy."

"*He* makes me happy."

"Then it's settled?"

"It's been settled."

"I want to show you something," Beverly said and left the room, returning with a bag made of a dirty, browned cloth and tied at the top with a worn red ribbon. Joy took the bag from her mother and opened it to discover a note, so thin and brittle it almost crumbled in her hands, and two small seeds. The note, folded many times to fit in the bag, read: "With this house, we plant not only our lives but our love. This bridal wreath, so easy to grow. Plant it and let it keep growing and growing and growing."

"Where'd this come from?" Joy asked, holding the note up to her face as if she was inspecting the paper's grain.

"Apparently, Mrs. Madson left it on the table near the door before she died. You know the one with the praying hands?"

Joy shivered. "Yeah."

"Did you know that house is over two hundred years old? Sydney at the office did some research on it when we were putting it up for sale."

"I always thought the Madsons were the original owners."

"Nope." Beverly took the seeds and rolled them around in the palm of her hand. "Bet she didn't start all those flower gardens either." They both laughed.

"I'm the only one at the office who knew the Madsons really well. You know they had no family, so all their belongings were donated to charity. This? Well, who would want it?"

Joy took the seeds from her mother and put them back in the cloth bag.

Chapter 19

Goldenrods

"**That** it?" Efram asked Joy as he stacked the last box next to a pet carrier for Mr. Boogie. Moving was a chore he abhorred. Most of his things were moved to a storage facility in Atlanta. With all the memories, he would not sell his Wenton home. It was their home now. Some of his belongings had been sent to New York, since he would be there for at least a month in the spring arranging the art show. It worked out perfectly, because Joy would be spending a month of the semester in Egypt on the dig. Part of their summer would be spent in New York with Efram's show, but he had promised Joy a special vacation anywhere in the world.

"That's everything. It's enough, though, especially with my things," Joy replied, staring at the pile of boxes, each carefully marked by Efram. The house was empty except for the painting, finished but covered with a cloth, sitting in the middle of the living room.

Efram looked around the room. "This place looks so big."

"It is big. Did you put the Egypt books in the car so I can read them on the drive up?"

"In the car."

"Can't wait, Ef!" She put her arms around him, lifting herself off the ground.

"Girl, you don't get out much. It's only Texas."

"No, Egypt! I can't believe I get to dig in Egypt! When the professor told me that, I almost flipped!"

"I know. You won't shut up about it!" He laughed and pointed towards the kitchen. "I have a surprise for you. Wait here." Opening his almost-empty refrigerator, he removed the food for their going-away meal.

He returned to the living room carrying a chilled bottle of grape juice and a box of mint Girl Scout cookies. Joy, sitting on the hardwood floor, rolled over laughing when she saw the cookies.

"Gee, Ef, you remembered! How'd you get those? It's not Girl Scout cookie season."

"I have many connections. It was hell infiltrating the Scouts, though." He sat down next to her and placed the items on the floor, then put champagne glasses in front of them. Shaking the bottle before opening it, he asked Joy to hold up the glasses for him to pour. Offering a toast, he said, "To nosy girls and smart-ass artists."

"Pardon? How 'bout to adventurous women and loony artists?"

"Like my version better."

They clicked their glasses and sipped the juice. Efram smiled and asked, "Cookie?"

"I'd rather see the painting."

"Sure you're ready?"

She nodded and they walked over to the canvas. Efram took a deep breath, but he wasn't nervous. With his hands on his hips, he walked around the painting like a drill sergeant about to give orders. Eyebrows raised, he looked at Joy, who was amused, and announced, "This is a momentous occasion." He thought about giving a long spiel, but seeing Joy standing there impatient, he decided to let the painting speak for itself and lifted the cover.

Uncovered, the canvas revealed a painting within a painting. In the portrait, Joy saw not only herself, seated on the window seat and wearing blue jeans and a T-shirt, she saw Efram at his easel, diligently painting them *both* on the window seat – she in her goddess outfit, he behind her in his favorite white silk shirt and black slacks. The floor in the tiny painting was covered with red roses, while that in the larger painting was covered with only the flower stains. The detail in the tiny portrait was incredible; Joy could see the trees at the window swaying.

"Oh, Efram, this is amazing!"

"*From a Vine*. That's the name."

"It's beautiful."

"I wanted to show it to you for Christmas, but it wasn't quite ready."

Joy pulled on the locket around her neck that held a tiny drawing of the two of them. On the back, it was inscribed "Ef and Joy forever."

"Now is the perfect time. Very symbolic," she said.

"I always wanted to make love to you on that window seat."

"What's stopping you now?"

He pulled her close and kissed her before carrying her to the spot where they had spent much of their time together. The window seat felt comfortable to Joy. Her back did not ache as Efram placed her lovingly on the cushions, nor did she feel a crick coming on in her neck. The only thing she missed was the *Heartsease* painting that used to hang across from her. As Efram kissed her earlobe, Joy said, "They didn't need a place to hide, Efram."

Efram looked up. "Who?"

"The lovers." Joy pointed at the blank wall.

Efram twisted his head, almost expecting to see the painting there. "No," he whispered and started kissing her again.

There were no curtains to block their passion, and they rolled to the floor and made love, the smell of the rose stains tingling their noses. For Efram, it was joy. For Joy, it was life.

As the day left the sky and the night took its rightful place in the heavens, Efram looked at Joy and knew that he had finally found passion, not about painting but about living, being. He had stopped paddling for once and let life flow, and it went exactly where he wanted it to. All the beauty he had tried so hard to capture, and sold for so much, was not small enough to be contained in any canvas. While Efram stared at her, Joy realized, as Mrs. Madson once told her, that passion is in your own backyard.

"Joy, I forgot something." Efram stood up and ran over to the canvas, naked. Joy smiled at the sight and followed him. "Paint! I need paint!" he yelled.

"Paint? It's all packed."

"Got a pen?" He looked ridiculous, standing there naked with his hands on his hips.

"A what?"

"Pen. You know, writing instrument."

Joy gave him the pen from her purse. With the black ink, he heavily etched "etc" at the bottom of the painting.

"Et cetera? Why'd you do that?"

"Efram Thomas Corbet. My initials."

"Your initials are et cetera?" Joy started laughing. "That's the funniest thing I've ever heard!"

Efram pulled her close and dipped her like they were starring in an old movie musical. "I just keep going and going and going."

With those words, he made love to her again. As he kissed her, he stopped to trace the scar on her upper lip with his tongue, removing any lingering pain.

~ ~ ~

The sky, dark as black velvet, held stars which glittered brighter than a ball gown. The night air was cold. The long tendrils of the willow trees swayed up and down like the skirts of a cancan dancer. Joy turned when she heard Efram step out onto the porch with two glasses of ice water. The water tasted good, but it did not cool them, even in the crisp December air. There was only one thing that could settle their souls before sleep. Watching the willow trees, Efram put down his glass on the porch railing. After placing Joy's glass next to his, he took her hand and led her into the yard, where they danced. He twirled her; she spun back into his arms. The cold dirt and dew-covered grass stuck to their bare feet with each step of their music-less waltz. A soft mound of freshly uprooted dirt clung to the balls of their feet. Earlier, they had planted Mrs. Madson's seeds. They were buried near the tree stump where Efram had parked his car and where Joy had played expedition leader as a child. Before long, as they danced, Joy stopped touching the ground, letting her feet dangle as her arms held on to Efram's shoulders. In bliss, her eyes closed, she rubbed her cheek against his. She felt his grin when his cheek muscles tightened.

"Your dancing has improved," Joy told him. Languid, she let her head fall back and looked at him.

Efram laughed through his nose. "Ever dance naked?"

Joy twisted her head and raised an eyebrow. "No."

"Up for it? It's like skinny-dipping in the air."

Joy smiled. "But what if someone sees?"

"Out here? I'm not expecting visitors, you know."

"Have you noticed it's kinda cold out here?"

"You're sweating, Joy."

They undressed, throwing their clothes in the air. Then Efram and Joy danced, giggling, drunk with love. When the moon was well hidden behind the trees of Wenton, Georgia, they slept, as quietly as the goldenrods waiting to sprout in the yard.

Michelle Cushing is a magna cum laude graduate with a Bachelor of Arts in journalism. She has published many articles and written numerous screenplays. Currently, she is working on her second novel.

For more information about the author and this book, log onto: www.fromavine.com

www.ingramcontent.com/pod-product-compliance
Lightning Source LLC
LaVergne TN
LVHW091546060526
838200LV00036B/728